Graceful

Graceful

WENDY MASS

SCHOLASTIC INC.

Copyright © 2015 by Wendy Mass

This book was originally published in hardcover by Scholastic Press in 2015.

All rights reserved. Published by Scholastic Inc., *Publishers since 1920*. SCHOLASTIC and associated logos are trademarks and/or registered trademarks of Scholastic Inc.

The publisher does not have any control over and does not assume any responsibility for author or third-party websites or their content.

No part of this publication may be reproduced, stored in a retrieval system, or transmitted in any form or by any means, electronic, mechanical, photocopying, recording, or otherwise, without written permission of the publisher. For information regarding permission, write to Scholastic Inc., Attention: Permissions Department, 557 Broadway, New York, NY 10012.

This book is a work of fiction. Names, characters, places, and incidents are either the product of the author's imagination or are used fictitiously, and any resemblance to actual persons, living or dead, business establishments, events, or locales is entirely coincidental.

ISBN 978-0-545-77314-0

10 9 8 7 6 5 4 3 2 1   17 18 19 20 21

Printed in the U.S.A.   40
First printing 2017

The text type was set in ITC Esprit.
Book design by Yaffa Jaskoll

For Grace, Amanda, Leo, Rory, Tara, Connor, and David, who let me know they had more to say

Dear my favorite reader (that's you!),

Writing the Willow Falls series these past few years has been a total joy. *The Last Present* was intended to be the last book. It even said so in the title! But it turns out Grace, Amanda, Leo, Rory, Tara, David, and Connor weren't ready to say good-bye. Plus, you guys made it VERY CLEAR that IN NO UNCERTAIN TERMS was the series allowed to end yet, and who am I to argue? If you're new to the series, it goes like this: *11 Birthdays, Finally, 13 Gifts, The Last Present*, and then this one, *Graceful*. If you haven't read the others, and you don't know why Rory hates bunnies or how Tara made her school principal cry or what happened to Amanda and Leo on that sandbar when they were stuck back in time, then you're probably not ready for *Graceful* yet.

But if you *do* know all those things, then I hope you'll enjoy seeing your old friends again. Thank you for welcoming them into your life in such an amazing way.

I've said it before, and I'll say it again, you guys ROCK! (Or as Grace would say, you guys are totes awesomesauce!)

xx,

Wendy

What is essential is invisible to the eye.
— from *The Little Prince* by Antoine de Saint-Exupéry

Vortex

Pronunciation: vawr-teks

Part of speech: noun

Plural form: **vor·tic·es, vor·tex·es**

Definition: **1.** a swirling mass of substance such as air, water, or fire. **2.** a spot from where a concentrated source of electromagnetic energy flows. **3.** a temporary doorway or portal to another level of existence.

Invisible lines of energy fling themselves across continents and oceans, and out to the farthest reaches of the galaxy. Where the lines cross, a vortex of energy sinks deep into the earth and waits. This concentrated energy contains all the possibilities in the universe, all the mathematical outcomes of your choices. If you were to stumble into it, you might feel a tingle, something you could blame on a cool breeze, or déjà vu. Or you might feel nothing at all. Our limited senses simply may not allow us to comprehend the true nature of reality. We think a tree is a tree. But if you look deeper, past the bark and the sap, into the molecules that make up the wood, deeper into the almost completely empty atom until you reach the smallest particles of matter, you will find only waves of energy. Not a solid "thing" at all. And those particles? They have no idea they're part of a tree. We, too, have no idea what we're a part of.

There are rumors of a select few who have come close to understanding, but they have not come forth to reveal themselves.

Chapter One

GRACE

"Admit it, if you suddenly had magical powers, you would have turned that leftover meat loaf into pizza, too."

Bailey shakes her head as we pedal down the uneven cobblestones of the hidden alley. "As much as I'm against your mom's meat loaf for many reasons," she says, "the first thing I would do if I had your powers is get straight A's on every report card."

"You already get straight A's," I point out.

She shakes her head. "Remember, I got that A-minus in gym last year for refusing to play dodgeball? Such a barbaric sport."

I pull to a stop in front of the last store on the right and swing down my kickstand. "Let me guess, *barbaric* was on your Word of the Day app today?"

"Yesterday," she says. "I've been waiting for an occasion to use it." She hops off her bike and lets it fall right over onto the street as she's done every time since we were six and learned to ride without training wheels. As the bike leaves her hands, I see it fall in slow motion, taking much longer to hit the ground than logic says it should. Time acting wonky is one of the weirdnesses that I've had to get used to ever since the vortex on the edge of town decided to pick *me* to share its power with when I turned ten. I hadn't asked for this gift, hadn't even known such a thing existed, but it's my destiny and I'm learning to live with it. The only people who know are my parents; my older brother, Connor; and a group of his friends who basically saved my life when they realized what was happening to me. They have now become my friends, too, which is very cool, because they are three years older and still want to hang out with me. They even call themselves Team Grace. I have a team!

I wasn't supposed to tell anyone else about the whole magical vortex thing, but Bailey's been my best friend ever since I started a petition in first grade to ban soda in the cafeteria, and she was the only person to sign it. She's crazy smart, and I know I can trust her.

"Ready?" Bailey asks as we approach the door of Angelina's Sweet Repeats and Collectibles. She pulls out the silk pouch where we keep the key to the store. It was Bailey's idea that such a special object shouldn't get shoved in a pocket or tossed in my bike basket. We made the pouch on my mom's sewing machine from the pants Connor wore the Halloween he was a pirate. Then we added glitter and sparkles because everything looks better with glitter and sparkles.

She hands me the key and steps back.

Breathe in, breathe out. Repeat. A few stray pieces of glitter waft down from my hand as I lift the key to the lock. I slip it in and take one more deep breath. Then I try to turn it to the right. It doesn't budge. To the left. Nothing. I lean my forehead against the cool glass door and my breath forms circles of fog.

It's been six weeks since my birthday. Every day I come here and try to get inside. Sometimes with Bailey, often with Connor and Team Grace. Once even with my parents, which was awkward, because they're still really freaked out by everything. Mom has already texted me nine times since Bailey and I left an hour ago.

But it doesn't matter what time of day or night it is, or who I'm with. The key never turns. The door never opens. All I can do is stare at all the clothes and toys and books and random *stuff* from the other side of a thick pane of glass. I wish I could use my power to open the door without the key, but I've tried and it doesn't work. I can only do small magical things, like changing that meat loaf into pizza, or making my parents lose track of time at the beach so we can stay longer.

Almost as soon as my powers came, they were gone. For a few days I could sense people's thoughts, and even make things move with a wave of my hand. That was fun. Made cleaning my room go a lot quicker! But now most of those things are gone. Angelina D'Angelo had the power of the vortex for a hundred years. I only had it for a week.

At first I'd tried to explain to the others how it felt to be able to see what I'd never imagined existed, like the way every person seemed connected to everyone else. Seeing the history of our town unfold in front of my eyes, it was like living a hundred years in seven days. I'm sure I didn't explain it well, though, and now it's slipping away from me, like a dream once you're fully awake.

But really, I shouldn't complain. I knew what would happen when Angelina and I combined our powers so we could cure Connor's best friend David's dad. Angelina had been trying to save him for decades from a really horrible disease, and she couldn't. But once I got my powers and added them to hers, we were strong enough. Doing it took all of Angelina's powers, and drained most of mine, too. She told me it will take mine two years to fully return.

Hers are gone for good. Secretly I worry that the most I'll ever be able to do is make pizzas. And I could have done that *without* magical powers!

I hand the key back to Bailey, who slips it into the pouch without a word.

"Maybe Angelina was just kidding when she gave me the key to her store before she left town," I say, sitting down on the hard cobblestones. I lean against the wall and cross my arms. "I mean, who leaves a whole store — probably full of magical stuff — to some fifth-grade kid?"

"You're not just *some* kid," Bailey says, sitting down beside me.

"Maybe I'm not the *right* kid, though. Maybe the vortex was supposed to choose someone else born in Willow Falls on the same day as me."

"Interesting," Bailey says. "I hadn't thought of that. *Was* anyone else born on the same day?"

I sigh. "No."

"Pretty sure it's you, then," she says. "You'll get more powerful soon."

"I don't know," I admit. "Angelina said she would help me build them back up, but I haven't heard a word since she left on the train. I know it's not her fault — she was stuck in Willow Falls for a hundred years. I mean, I love our town and all, but that would make anyone want to leave. Maybe there's something in the store that's supposed to help me."

"Can you track her down and tell her the key isn't working?"

I shake my head. "She could be on the other side of the world for all I know. Now school starts in a few days, and I'll have to pretend to be a normal person again while all this is going on in my head."

Bailey pats my leg. "You were never normal, if that makes you feel any better."

"Not really."

"What are you girls doing here?" a deep voice asks. "This is private property, you know." We look up in surprise, but the glare from the sun hides the man's face. We scramble to our feet. I haven't seen a single other person come down this alley all summer. Maybe we're not supposed to be here!

"Ray!" Bailey says, recognizing him first. She punches him on the arm. "We thought we were in trouble!"

Ray grins. "Couldn't resist," he says, returning to his usual Australian accent. "Your mugs just looked so serious."

Ray is on Team Grace, but mostly he just drives us places and does stuff we need a grown-up to do. Bailey and

I totally had crushes on him when he directed the play we were in last month. Once Jake Harrison showed up, though, we quickly forgot about Ray. Ray's old, anyway! Like, at least twenty-four! Jake's only fourteen and is *soooooo* talented and cute and is super nice for a big-time movie star. But he only has eyes for Connor's friend Rory, and since Rory is totes awesomesauce, we need to find new crushes.

"Pretty brave of you to try to scare us," I say, climbing onto my bike. "I could have turned you into a turtle. Angelina did that once to her brother who was being annoying. Then you would have had to go home to Australia for Christmas and explain to your family why you're moving so slowly."

He laughs. "Yikes. I thought all you could do was change things into pizzas."

I squint up at him. "Where'd you hear that?"

"Your bro Connor may have let it slip when he came to work at the house last week."

"Is Connor making actual money working for Tara's uncle?" Bailey asks.

"No," Ray says. "He's getting paid in magic beans. Of course he's getting real money!"

"I wouldn't mind some of those magic beans," I mutter.

"Patience, little one," he says, patting me on the head. "I'm betting in no time at all you'll be making pizzas left and right."

I swat at him.

"Crikey! Almost forgot the reason I'm here." He reaches into his back pocket. "Connor asked me to give you this. It came to your house in the mail this mornin'."

He places a postcard in my hand. It's a picture of a circle of giant stones standing up in a field. The words *Greetings from . . . Stonehenge!* are splashed across the front. I flip it over. "It's from Angelina!" I announce. "She really *is* on the other side of the world!"

Bailey leans over my shoulder. "She finally gets in touch with you, and the only thing she writes on the postcard is your address? That's annoying."

I look up at her. "What do you mean?"

"I mean, it's blank," Bailey says.

"No, it's not," I reply.

Chapter Two

GRACE

"*Yes, it is,*" she and Ray say together.

"No, it's not," I repeat. "You guys really can't see the writing on it?"

They shake their heads.

I don't want to be rude by smiling, but if I can see something they can't, that means I do still have some real magic left in me. Angelina had said we would have a special link, and I guess she was right.

"What does it say, then?" Bailey asks.

"I have no idea," I admit. "It's written in some kind of code."

Ray chuckles. "That Angelina. Looks like giving up her powers hasn't changed her much."

"What kind of code?" Bailey asks.

"It's a whole bunch of weird symbols and tiny pictures in a circular pattern. Let's go back to my house and I'll write it out for you."

* * * * * * * * * * *

Two hours later, Bailey and I are sitting at my kitchen table with the rest of Team Grace — Amanda, Leo, Rory, Tara, David, and Connor. I haven't seen much of David lately since he almost never leaves his dad's side, so it makes me feel good that he came for me. My mom is hovering over by the stove not even bothering to pretend she isn't listening to us.

Rory leans over to me and whispers, "Is your mom okay? She looks a little *gray* sort of?"

I know what she means. "I don't think she sleeps much," I reply. "Whenever I wake up at night, the light is always on in their room."

"I wish there was something we could do so your parents wouldn't worry so much," Rory says. "But after everything they've been through, I can't really blame them."

Leo bangs an old rubber mallet (we couldn't find a gavel) on the table and says, "An official meeting of Team Grace is now called to order." Leo has become the unofficial spokesman for the group. Connor gave him his mallet to use at meetings. Now that Connor's gotten a job helping Tara's uncle, an inventor, he gets to keep all of Mr. St. Claire's old tools. I think our parents should focus less on me, and pay more attention to the fact that Connor has dismantled most of the electronic devices in our house, our old lawn mower, and basically any object that has more than one part.

"First order of business," Leo says. "Grace's postcard from Angelina. Now, Grace, will you show us what you —"

"You got a postcard from Angelina?" Mom asks, cutting him off. She rushes over to the table, clenching and unclenching her hands. That's only *one* of the new nervous habits she's developed.

I look at Connor. "You didn't tell Mom about the postcard?" As soon as I ask, I already know the answer. Connor tries to shelter our parents from all this stuff whenever possible. I should have realized he wouldn't have mentioned it.

"Is that it?" Mom asks, pointing at the postcard in the center of the table.

No one answers, but it's pretty obvious. She reaches for the card, stares down at the giant rock circle, then flips it over.

"Oh!" she says in surprise. "It's blank."

"Yes!" I say, with perhaps a bit too much excitement. I'd actually forgotten that she wouldn't be able to see the writing.

She drops it back on the table and says, "Hopefully that woman is gone for good. Maybe she'll settle down in England."

The rest of us nod and murmur *maybe* and *probably*, but I'm pretty sure no one thinks Angelina is truly gone from Willow Falls. She's a part of this town.

I focus on sending Mom a suggestion and then wait for her to speak. A few seconds later, she says, "Why don't you kids go play outside? With school starting next week, you should get all the fresh air you can."

It worked! Now I can show them what I copied down without Mom hearing us. Everyone hurries to their feet.

"Wait!" she says. We freeze. Uh-oh! Did I mess up and send all my thoughts to her? Does she know we're trying to get away from her? I really need Angelina to teach me how to do this stuff! I hold my breath, but to my surprise she turns to Leo. "Would you like to use the bathroom first?" she asks. "Before you start playing and lose track of time and then it's too late?"

"Um, I think I'm good?" he says, his cheeks turning a cute shade of red.

"Having a weak stomach is nothing to be embarrassed about," she says. "Your friends all understand, right?"

Tara and Rory quickly turn their heads away so my mom can't see their faces. Amanda says, "It's okay, Mrs. Kelly. I made sure Leo went before he left home today. Your bathroom is safe for another day."

My mom shrugs. "Well, just in case, I put extra toilet paper in there."

We run outside to the backyard and Amanda, Tara, and Rory totally crack up. I don't know all the details of the Leo-stuck-in-the-bathroom story because that was during the week Angelina had put me in a coma and I couldn't understand anything going on around me. But the story had something to do with a bad burrito and a *lot* of toilet paper. Must have been really funny because Tara is now wiping her eyes with the bottom of her orange T-shirt. "We'll tell you later," Rory promises Bailey and me.

Leo bangs his mallet on the side of a tree. Since it's rubber, it makes pretty much no sound. He waves his arms instead. "All right, all right," he says. "I know it's hilarious that Mrs. Kelly thinks I clogged up her toilet, but we have more important things to focus on." He holds out his hand to me. "Do you have the code?"

I pull a folded piece of notebook paper out of my pocket

and hand it to him. "I traced it," I explain as he kneels down and spreads it out on our patio. The others gather around him.

One by one the members of Team Grace gasp and turn pale. "This outer circle is about me!" Amanda says. "Me and Leo."

Rory points to the middle ring. "And this is me!"

Tara wordlessly points to the circle inside Rory's.

I peer closer at the outer ring. All I see is a string of pictures: an apple, a duck, a candle, a cake, a potted plant, a bee, a lollipop, a football, a lizard, a drum, and then something square with eyes. "What's that one?" I ask.

Amanda shudders. "That's SpongeBob SquarePants."

I look up, confused. "I don't get it. What does a cartoon character have to do with the two of you?"

Leo picks up the paper. "All of the things in this circle have something to do with our eleventh birthday. The one where we met Angelina for the first time."

"Look, David," Amanda says, pointing to the tiny picture of the bee. "That's you!"

They all laugh, and I don't bother to ask why it's funny. Willow Falls is full of stories, most of them known only to a few. I got to see glimpses of them when I first got my powers, but now I only see an occasional flash when I sense a connection between two people. The older members of

Team Grace each have a glowing, white light around them, and when they are all together like this, the lights reach for one another until the air pulses with a golden glow. These are the kinds of things I keep to myself.

"Do you think this means Angelina's not done with us yet?" Tara asks, the paper in her hand shaking.

I can see the fear in her eyes. From what I've learned of her story, out of everyone on Team Grace, she had it the hardest. She and her family had to move every few years because Angelina kept finding them. Finally Tara was forced to come to Willow Falls to stay with relatives she barely knew, and then the craziness *really* began. Now her family is moving here, and she's looking forward to a fresh start. One that *doesn't* include Angelina.

I stare down at the circle. The pattern reminds me of something, but I can't think what it is. I close my eyes and reach deep down inside me, feeling around for the tiny magical spark resting there. I take a few deep breaths and focus harder. I can feel the spark like a lightning bug buzzing and zigzagging inside, warming me up and connecting me with a power greater than myself.

Suddenly I know two things for certain. First, Angelina *is* done with the others, but I'm not. They're a part of something big that's coming, but it's not today. It's not this month. But it's coming.

And second, I need to do whatever it takes to get my full powers back, because when that big thing comes, I have to be ready to protect Willow Falls and everyone in it. I focus on the light within me, willing it to tell me more. It only twinkles and fades out.

When I open my eyes, Team Grace is happily munching on a steaming, fresh pizza that has suddenly appeared on the picnic table. I know there's no chance a pizza delivery guy dropped it off while I had my eyes closed. Leo and David are holding two slices each and grinning.

"That is one handy talent, Grace!" Leo says, his mouth full of gooey cheese.

I join them at the table and rest my head in my hands. Willow Falls is in big trouble.

AMANDA

Dear Diary,

Well, the strangest summer of my life is now over. And that's saying a lot considering a few years ago I was stuck in my eleventh birthday for eleven days!! Still, I think traveling back in time out-weirds being stuck in time. Or maybe it's a tie!

I'm sure I wasn't the only one today who was relieved when Grace told us that she won't need us for a while, even though I feel a little guilty. Getting to be a part of the turnover of power from Angelina to Grace was an awesome experience, and I'm totally honored and all that, but I need to catch up with my real life. Like, Kylie invited me to go running with her in the mornings, and since it's the first time my sister has asked me to do ANYTHING with her since we were little kids, I said yes. So now I have to get running shoes. And last-minute school supplies. Also, Stephanie's having her thirteenth birthday party tonight — a swimming party — and I'm nervous since it's mostly her gymnastics friends. Being a drummer in the school marching band has not upped my coolness factor. Having a boyfriend might, but I'm definitely not telling any of Stephanie's friends about me and Leo. I just don't know if I'm ready to be an official "girlfriend." It sounds so grown-up. Leo always wants to "talk about our relationship," but I keep changing the subject. It's like all he thinks about. I know that's supposed to be what I should want. Ugh, SOOOO confused. I think I just need a break.

School starts in two days!!! I can't wait to see if I'm in any classes with anyone from Team Grace. Well, of course Grace and Bailey won't be in my classes, but I'll still see them at school. Bailey's a good kid, or a "good egg" as my dad would say. Going through what Grace is going through without a best friend by her side would be awful. I wish I had told Stephanie what was happening on my eleventh birthday while I was still going through it, but I was afraid of how she'd react. Grace is much braver than me, in many ways. I guess she has to be. I don't think I'd want to be in her shoes, but she seems to be taking it pretty well.

If someone told me that a vortex of magic energy had selected me, the one person in a hundred years, to protect a whole town, I'm pretty sure I'd be hiding under my bed right now.

Kylie was right when she said writing things down would help me sort out my feelings. I think it's helping. She gave you to me on my eleventh birthday, and I shoved you and your shiny purple cover in a drawer, and kinda forgot about you. Sorry, Diary!!

TTYL,

Me / Amanda / Drummer Girl / Girlfriend of Leo's (not sure) / Best friend of Leo's (always. At least I hope.)

LEO

Ode to Magic Pizza
By Leo Fitzpatrick

O magic pizza, you are so yummy,
Now you are sitting in my tummy,
I swear you taste better than the real stuff,
Almost like you were made with Marshmallow Fluff!
Mmmm, fluff!
Fluffernutter sandwiches are the best,
And I have tried all the rest! But this poem is about
Magic Pizza, which I will miss a ton,
Because Grace kicked us out
Of all the fun.

She must want to keep you all to herself,
Nah, I'm just kidding, but it will be rough.
I'll miss Team Grace and especially "A,"
But I know I'll still see her every day,
Because now she's my girlfriend . . . Yay!

RORY

Rory: OMG!!! You are my first real text with my first real keyboard!!!!

Jake: Your parents finally gave in?

It took all my babysitting $ from the whole summer but I got it! I can even get pictures! It's all very exciting!! :D times infinity! Sorry, that came out sounding way girly.

Well, you ARE a girl after all! That's what I like about you, it doesn't take much to make you happy! ;-)

True. So where are you right now?

Backstage at my LAST D&P!! Huzzahh!!

D&P?

Oh sorry! Stands for Dog and Pony show. It's where the cast tries to impress the people interviewing us so they want to be our best friends and say nice things about our movie.

Have fun!

I'd rather be hanging out in your strange town with you and your strange family and strange friends. ;-)

LOL, my town and my family are definitely strange, but my friends are pretty normal.

Dunno, I'm pretty sure two of them disappeared into thin air at the beach last month.

. . . erp . . . um . . .

Just kidding, didn't mean to freak you out! gtg, thing starting. oo, J

. . . .

Rory: SO you'll never guess what Jake just said.

Amanda: Um, that he loves you and he's leaving life in the spotlight for a peaceful, quiet existence in Willow Falls?

Haha. No. He joked about seeing you and Leo disappear at the beach last month.

That's weird. If he saw us, why did he pretend not to? I mean he's a good actor but i don't think he's that good!

I think his brain is trying to make sense of it.

Hey, this is a long text for you. Did u FINALLY get a normal phone???

Yup!! Love it!!!!!

Did Jake sign his text with the two o's again? Someday you'll change one to an x! ;o)

I'm sure he'll come to his senses before then and some other girl will get those x's. Someone much cooler and cuter.

No one is cooler and cuter than Rory Swenson, the pirate with the elephant ear. ;o)

Speaking of kisses . . . how's that coming with Leo?

Gtg! Bye!

Um, Amanda?

Hellooooo?

I know you're still seeing these!

No i'm not.

LOL. See you in school tomorrow.

TARA

Dear Julie,

I'm sorry it's taken me six weeks to write back since you sent your (FIFTEEN-PAGE!!) letter, but hey, better than the four years it took me last time!! And now you only have to read one letter, instead of all sixty-seven, so, bonus for you! I loved reading about everything that's been going on in your life in the last four years!! I thought about you all the time, even though you didn't know it. Rapunzel = a great name for a dog! I remember how you used to beg for one when we were little! I'm glad your parents worked things out, too, and that your brother is getting better. I'm enclosing two comic books in this envelope for him that my uncle gave me from his collection. Remind me to tell you one day about all the things he collects.

It's taken me this long to reply to your letter because knowing that you actually read ALL THOSE LETTERS that I had written to you but never mailed kinda threw me for a loop. It was my cousin Emily who sent them. She found where I hid them and didn't even ask. I know she was trying to be nice (I think!!) but it kind of feels like someone stole my diary and sent it across the country. You know all my secrets now. Thank you for still wanting to be my friend after reading all that! And thank you for saying that we're real friends now, not just pen pals like before, and for forgiving the fact that I just disappeared on you. Even though I wasn't mailing the letters, writing them still made me feel close to you. Sounds crazy, I know. Now you're the only person who really knows me, or I should say *knew* me, because I've definitely changed since I've been here. I can tell as I'm writing this that it sounds different from my other letters, and not just the words, the way I feel while writing them.

After I got your letter, I realized that if I want to be close with the new friends I've made since coming to Willow Falls, I had to tell them about my life before I got here. I mean, they knew I didn't have a lot of friends (okay, any really), but I finally told them the kinds of things I told you in the letters, about being lonely and how riding my bike gave me freedom, and stuff about my parents and their relationship. Then I finally came clean about the goat and the pepper spray, and repeating the story out loud kind of made it seem funny and not so tragic, and the fact that they were laughing so hard they were crying helped a bit, too!

So as you know from letter #67 that I wrote right after the "Goat / Pepper Spray Incident," I was sent away to stay with my cousin Emily (two years younger than you and me) and her parents (Aunt Bethany and Uncle Roger, who is a kind of famous inventor). They already had a houseguest, a cute/tan/friendly/strange (but good strange) guy from Australia named Ray who wants to be an actor — he used to be Uncle Roger's assistant, but now he's busy starting up the community theatre program here. Ray and Emily looked out for me when I first got here, even when I tried to keep to myself. But then remember how I complained in my letters how my mom always made us move all the time? Well, after I was here a few weeks, I found out why! It has to do with something my mom did when she was a kid. It's a LONG story, and there are parts of it that I can't talk about yet, but basically, my family got a lot closer because of it, so it had a happy ending.

To tell you a little about my friends, the first person I met was this girl Amanda, who is very friendly and kind of marches to the beat of her own drum. I mean literally, she plays drums in the school marching band! That takes guts, right? She's also kind of wise beyond her years, like she's seen some *stuff*! She is dating this boy named Leo who she was best friends with since the day they were born, so that's a little weird for her, I think. Leo is super nice, and he and I hit it off really easily. The other kids tease him about writing poems, but if he really does write them, I've never seen any.

Then I met Rory, who became friends with Amanda and Leo a year ago. She also babysits my cousin Emily, even though Emily can totally take care of herself. I've never met anyone like Rory. Sometimes it's almost as if she's not there, like she blends into the background, but not on purpose, like the way I used to do it. But then other times — most times — she's like this bright light, like a flame that people are drawn to because she's so, I don't know, innocent or something? Trusting? Thoughtful? She's also funny and clumsy, and here's the most AMAZING part: she's doing this almost-dating thing with . . . hold on . . . you'll never believe it . . . Jake Harrison!! I think it's a secret, though, so please, please don't tell anyone. You know that new movie he's in, *Playing It Cool*, that just came out a few weeks ago? He filmed it right here!! Rory and a whole bunch of other kids in town got to be extras. Jake is super, super cool and nice and not at all movie-starry, if you can get past all the screaming fans and camera flashes going off. I thought I would die of embarrassment when my dad told him I used to kiss his poster every night before bed. I'm hoping there was too much noise at the premiere of the movie and he didn't hear that! Yes, I met Jake!!! A few times, actually. He sang in a play that I produced. Yes, I produce plays now!!!!! Told you I've changed!!!! It was a one-time thing, though, that's for sure!! I'm sure I've used more exclamation points so far in this letter than in all sixty-seven combined!!!

Next I met a boy named Connor who works for my uncle because he wants to be an inventor when he grows up. He calls me New Girl even though I've lived here in Willow Falls now almost two months, but I kind of like it. I've never had a nickname before. At least not one that people called me to my face! ;o) Connor has a younger sister named Grace, who has a lot of responsibility for someone her age, and we've all agreed to help her whenever she needs us. Yup, I help people now, too! LOL. And I say things like LOL. And sometimes even "like" and "OMG." I know, embarrassing, right? I think I just want to sound like everyone else.

So the only person I haven't mentioned yet is Connor's best friend, David, who lives across the street from my aunt and uncle. He's tall like me, so I don't feel like a giant next to him like I do next to most kids our age. He is really smart and kind of anxious sometimes, but also really easygoing, and has this amazing voice when he sings outside. He's kind of deep, ya know? Like an onion. I mean, in the way that there are layers to him that I'm still finding. Much more about him to tell, but that will have to wait for the next letter because my mom is dragging me out for school supplies because we're moving here! And STAYING!!! Mom swears it this time!! So tomorrow I start yet another new school, but this time I'll have friends before I even start. Me = very excited and kind of embarrassed that I'm so excited!!

w/b/s and I promise I will, too!!!

XO

Tara, your old pen pal / friend

PS: Thank you for saying my letters were better than any book you've read. I doubt that, but it made me feel good!

DAVID

Dear David,

We at OFT (Online Family Therapy) are looking forward to working with you as you adjust to this new phase of your family's life together. Please answer the following questions honestly and openly. It will help us help you! Your mother believes you could benefit from our help and you can rest assured that your responses will be kept completely confidential.

Q: Tell us a little about yourself.

A: My name is David. I'm thirteen. Just had my bar mitzvah. I wear glasses, which I don't mind because they make me look smarter. I like to sing. I like hanging out with my best friend, Connor, and other friends like Rory, Amanda, and Leo. I want to be a pediatrician when I grow up. I have a brand-new girlfriend named Tara, which I never thought I'd have. I mean, I never thought I'd have a girlfriend, not that I never thought I'd have one named Tara. You know what I mean. She and her family just moved in down the street from me. I liked her from the first time I looked up at her from the bottom of an empty pool hole. She is almost as tall as me, and I think she is very pretty even though she doesn't think about stuff like what she wears or makeup or hair like some other girls. She says what's on her mind (usually). She's also independent and a deep thinker. We "get" each other. We've both had really bizarre experiences, and things like that can bond you for life. I don't get to see her as much now that my dad's home, but she totally understands.

Q: How do you feel about your father returning home after so many years in the hospital and special clinics?

A: Are you kidding? I'm still jumping up and down like a kid seeing snow for the first time.

Q: How is your father adjusting to life at home?

A: Great! We're doing all sorts of fun things together to make up for lost time. Swimming, playing ball, long walks, and a lot of eating! It's awesome. Usually it's awesome. I mean, well, some days I guess it's a little hard for him to be this big "medical miracle." The doctors from his old clinic keep calling and asking about his overnight recovery, and my dad can't blame them because he knows they want to help their other patients, but he doesn't know what to tell them. All he knows is that one day he was completely healed. Sometimes he doesn't want to leave the house, like he feels guilty or something, but then he's usually okay after a bit.

Also, he has to get used to how my mom runs things and our routine and everything, and I think it's hard because he feels like he should be back at work, but my mom wants him to rest more. I don't want him to go to work yet, either. In fact, I should go check on him. Okay, I'm back. He's all good. I told him I'd put air in our bike tires, and he said I didn't have to, but I'm hoping if there is air in the tires he will agree to ride.

Q: If you have any questions for us, or about this process, please ask below.

A: Why is the sky blue? Just kidding. Although actually not kidding, I really don't know.

End of new patient questionnaire. Thank you for your time.

You're welcome, I guess. I'm not really sure why my mother thinks I need to do this, but I'm not in the mood to complain about anything right now, so I'm just going with the flow, dude. That's something my friend Connor would say.

CONNOR

CONNOR KELLY'S INVENTOR'S JOURNAL

Type of product: Hands-Free Umbrella

Inventor: Roger St. Claire, Connor Kelly (assistant)

Description of invention-in-progress: Hands-free umbrella to protect the user from rain, snow, or sunlight.

What problem does it solve: Allows the user to carry items in both hands while still being protected by an umbrella, or to carry items in one hand — a phone, a camera, groceries — and hold a child's hand with the other.

Who will want or need this product: Everyone who likes to keep dry without the burden of holding an umbrella with his or her hand!

Materials: acrylic coating, microfiber, rayon, Lycra, nylon, Scotchgard finish, steel, aluminum, wood, plastic, wire, metal hinges, metal springs, adjustable denim straps, rare earth magnets

Steps: Experiment with positioning the tops of umbrellas by clipping onto hat, resting on shoulders, attaching to backpack or headband. Underarm straps? Magnetized to jacket?

Results: After much trial and error (mostly consisting of Connor Kelly trying on various prototypes and then having a garden hose aimed at his head while he juggled tennis balls), the best solution was deemed to be a flexible coil that attaches to the bottom of a regular umbrella stem and is then wound around the wearer's shoulder and tucked under his or her arm to hold into place, as shown below:

Final observations: For this inventor's assistant, getting to be a part of inventing the **Hands-Free Umbrella Snake** was an amazing experience. I got to see how an invention is first dreamed up by an existing need, and then how many options are considered and attempted before the best solution is found. And the best is often the simplest.

Chapter Three

GRACE

I've been back at school exactly three days, and I have been sent to the principal's office FOUR TIMES! And none of it was my fault! I underestimated how quickly word of me being in the hospital over the summer had spread. Even though they don't know what really happened, everybody at school knows I was sick, even the teachers! Kids in Willow Falls almost never go to the hospital (thanks to Angelina's magic), so whenever I walk down the hall (or sit in class or eat lunch or change for gym), kids point at me like I'm a circus freak. I'm causing a distraction just by existing, at least that was the reason for my first two trips.

Then on Wednesday afternoon, I was accused of

cheating because I finished the math assignment in only two minutes when it should have taken twenty. It really *did* feel like twenty minutes to me, and when I argued this, the teacher showed me the clock. I wish Angelina had warned me about this wonky time stuff. Last night I almost flooded the house when I turned on the bath water and then, in what seemed like only seconds later, the tub was overflowing.

My final trip to see the principal (who I'm now getting to know very well) was actually MOM'S fault! We're only allowed to have phones at school if they're turned off, but Mom turned mine on this morning without telling me because she didn't like that she couldn't reach me from nine till three each day. So of course it rings during the Pledge of Allegiance, which is (according to my teacher) not only rude but also unpatriotic.

Principal Rees decided it was time for a little chat with my parents, so now I'm sitting in the hall outside his office waiting for Mom to arrive. I look up from doodling in my social studies notebook to see that an older boy has joined me in the hallway. He leans against the opposite wall outside the nurse's office. His arm is all bandaged up. "Yo," he says.

"Yo," I reply. "Skateboard accident?"

He shakes his head. "My bunny tried to kill me. Again."

I've practiced lifting one eyebrow for just this type of occasion. I lift it. "Really? A killer bunny? You don't hear that very often."

He shrugs.

A series of pictures suddenly flashes across my mind, like watching a movie on super-fast-forward. *The mall. A cage. A bunny with orange ears. Rory! A magician. The ceramic bunny Leo made Connor when I was sick.* "Kyle!" I blurt out.

The kid looks up from examining his arm, surprised. "How do you know his name?"

I smile. "He has a long history of unstable behavior. You may want to lock him in another room when you go to sleep."

"Tried that," the boy says.

"Grace!" Mom rushes down the hall toward us, out of breath and pale. "Is everything all right?"

Mom gives the boy a quick glance as he ducks into the nurse's office.

"Bunny attack," I explain.

"Why are *you* here?" she asks. My old mom — the one who I had before the vortex turned our lives upside down, the one who I could laugh with and tell anything to, who I could shop with and dance to pop music with — would have at least smiled at the idea of an evil bunny. But the new post-vortex version of my mother doesn't seem to have a sense of humor anymore.

I close my notebook and get to my feet. I don't want to worry her. "It's no big deal," I tell her. "Just taking a little longer to adjust to school."

She wrings her hands. "You promised you were going to be a normal girl as much as possible, at least while you could."

"I know. It's not always up to me."

She frowns. "I'm sorry about calling your phone this morning. This was supposed to be my first day back at work, but then, I don't know, I couldn't go." Her eyes get glossy and she looks down.

The principal's door opens and he ushers us inside. I swallow the lump in my throat. Mom loves her part-time job at the local newspaper, and I had hoped returning to work would help her get back to her old self.

I only half listen as the principal tells my mother that they're all very pleased I am fully recovered from whatever led to my hospital stay, and that they will help me to adjust any way they can. Guess I'm not in trouble. Mom looks relieved, but the dark circles under her eyes from lack of sleep are still as dark. I have accepted my destiny and the responsibilities that will one day go along with it. But for my parents, there's just too much worry.

Her voice cracks as she thanks the principal, and something cracks within me. My heart starts beating faster, and I feel that little spark inside me grow warmer. I take a deep breath, and it grows warmer still. That's interesting. I take another, deeper breath, and now I can feel the energy inside me build. I glance at the little silver clock on the edge of the principal's desk just in time to see the second hand jerk to a stop.

I blink and look again. It hasn't budged. Then I look around me. Mom and Principal Rees look like they're in a movie that just froze on the screen, the characters stuck in midsentence.

I jump up from my chair and run out into the hall. The hallway is completely empty except for a girl kneeling on the floor, stopped in the middle of yanking a sweatshirt out of her locker. I watch to see if she's going to stand. She doesn't. I stand still for a few minutes, not sure what to do. Then the echo of footsteps pounding the floor reaches me from both directions. One after the other, the members of Team Grace round the corners of the hallways and I breathe a sigh of relief that I'm not in this alone. Leo reaches me first. "Where is it?" he asks, peeking around behind me. He's like an eager puppy trying to find a hidden bone.

"Where's what?"

"The pizza!"

I would laugh, but I'm too freaked out. "No pizza this time, sorry."

He pretends to pout, then says, "Oh well! What's going on, then?"

Connor reaches us before I can answer. He throws his arms around me. "Are you okay? What's happening?"

I untangle myself from his arms as the girls reach us. Tara and Rory are laughing about something on Rory's phone, and Amanda looks, well, kind of annoyed, actually. She quickly rearranges her face, but I saw what I saw.

"Well, this is different," Connor declares. "I was sitting in math class and Mr. Nelson had just announced a pop quiz and I was like, dude, on the third day of school? Really? And then everyone suddenly froze in the middle of whatever they were doing. The kid behind me was midsneeze and all these gross droplets of snot just hung in the air. And if it grossed *me* out, you know it was gross. Then it was like I knew right where to find you. I think this may be the weirdest thing that's ever happened to me."

Tara pats Connor on the shoulder. "Oh, you poor, delusional boy. This isn't even *close* to the weirdest thing that's going to happen to you."

"Thanks, New Girl," he says. "I'm not sure if that's good or bad."

"Where's David?" Amanda asks.

We all look around. No David.

"I don't know his schedule yet," Tara says. "Maybe history class? Or is it art?"

"We should try to find him," Amanda says. "This is the first time he's experienced magic like this. He might be totally freaking out. I know I was when it happened to me."

"You're right," Leo says, suddenly serious. "It can be really scary the first time. Especially when you're alone." He reaches for Amanda's hand. Is it my imagination, or does she flinch for a split second before taking it?

"Or . . ." Rory says, "what if David's frozen like everyone else? Maybe he's not able to feel the magic after all. Maybe once his dad came home, his part in all this was over?"

No one answers. Tara looks like someone punched her. She turns to me and says, "That would be awful. He was left out of everything that happened with me when I first came here, and then he was away when you were in your coma thing, and he so badly wants to help you after everything you did for his dad. If he —"

But she doesn't get to finish her thought. The door to a

bathroom a few feet away from us suddenly swings open. Out walks David, tucking in his shirt. He stops when he sees us, then grins. "Hey, guys! What are you all doing out here?"

Tara runs up and throws her arms around him. His glasses go flying off. Amanda runs over and hands them to him. "Now *this* feels familiar!" she says.

"Wow," David says, sliding his glasses back on. "If I knew I'd get a hug every time I came out of the bathroom, I'd chug water all day long! But, seriously, did I miss the memo about cutting class?"

Tara takes him by the arm and leads him to the doorway of the closest classroom. She points inside.

"I don't get it," David says after a few seconds. "Why aren't they moving?"

"Grace stopped time," Tara says plainly.

"Say what now?" he replies. He looks around at the rest of us.

"It's true," Connor says. "Crazy, right, Hamburglar? My little sister can stop time!"

I feel a tingle of pride, but mostly fear. I blurt out, "What if I can't start it again?"

Rory puts her hand on my shoulder. "Why don't you tell us what happened."

I explain about the trips to the principal, and how my mom is here, and about how I can't stand the way all this is affecting my parents. Then I get to the part about the clock stopping, and as the words leave my mouth, I realize the connection. "I know! Right when I made the decision that I had to do something for my parents, time stopped."

"But what can you do?" David asks. "You can't make them forget it all happened. Or can you? I don't really understand how any of this works."

"I . . . I don't know if I can," I admit. "I don't even know where I'd begin."

"Angelina used to make potions a long time ago," Tara says. "Maybe there's one for making people forget."

"But it wouldn't just be our parents," Connor points out. "It would have to be everyone who knew about Grace going to the hospital, which in this town is practically everyone. And the hospital staff, too."

"You're right," I say. "But how would I possibly be able to do that?"

"You stopped TIME!" Rory points out. "And you don't even have most of your powers back."

"Good point," I admit.

"Let's go to Angelina's house after school," Tara

suggests. "She has a huge herb garden in the front yard. Maybe you can figure out how to combine them in the right way or something."

"I don't think we're supposed to wait that long," Leo says, pointing behind us. I turn around to see Ray striding down the hall toward us.

"Where to?" he asks, holding up his keys.

Chapter Four

GRACE

Five minutes later, we're all piled into Ray's car and heading onto Main Street.

"I would have taken the boss's SUV," he explains, "but it wouldn't turn on. Only my little guy worked."

"It's okay," I tell him. "And I'm sorry about all this. I'm sure you were in the middle of something."

"No worries, mate," he says. "I've seen stranger things."

"This is like Frogger!" Connor shouts as our car darts between all the cars stopped dead in the road.

I'm sitting on Connor's lap in the back, squished between David and Rory. My mind is shooting in all directions. How did I do this? Do I even have the right to do this?

"Are you okay?" Rory asks.

I shake my head. "I keep thinking about how the whole world is stopped right now," I tell her. "Babies are in the middle of being born, couples are in the middle of getting married. Airplanes are in the middle of takeoff!" I shiver. "Isn't this dangerous? Or wrong somehow, to play with people's lives who we don't even know?"

Amanda turns around from the front seat. "I don't think it works that way. Leo and I had a lot of time to think about it over the last few years. I think what happens when you or Angelina stops time is that it's not like time is actually *stopped*, like someone pressed the PAUSE button on the world. It's more like you opened up a crack in time, and we slipped inside. We're the ones in a place with no time, not them. So from their point of view, nothing has changed. Does that make sense?"

I go over her words in my head as I look out the car window at the world frozen around us. The leaves are stuck mid-sway, the birds mid-glide. "So basically, I didn't stop time at all, I just pulled us out of it."

"Exactly," Amanda says, smiling warmly.

I return her smile, glad that she seems back to normal. Maybe she had been in the middle of a really good class before, and that's why she'd been annoyed in the hallway.

. . . .

Angelina's house looks totally different from what I'd expected. Actually, I don't know what I'd expected. It's hard to picture her living anywhere as ordinary as a house. But I know we're at the right place, not only because of the GO AWAY sign or the strong smell of apples or the neatly labeled herb and flower gardens, but because I can see her everywhere. There she is leaning over the birdbath; there she is picking a basketful of thistle and a pinch of rosemary.

I can hear her talking to herself, too, calculating how much she needs of this or that, and whether to boil, grind, or blend it into a cream. I can see her rushing about with long brown hair streaming behind her, and swinging on a porch rocker that is no longer here. Sometimes a young version of Bucky is by her side, and they are talking and laughing or sometimes arguing, but mostly she's alone. Her hair gradually turns white as snow as season after season flies by in a blur.

I shake my head to get rid of the ghostly images. It doesn't work. Tara is talking to me, so I force myself to focus on what she's saying.

"My mom has been taking care of the gardens since a few days after Angelina left," she says. "I help her sometimes, so if you tell me what you need, I can show you where it is."

"I thought your mom hated Angelina?" Leo asks her.

"Don't say *hate*," Rory and Tara reply at the same time.

"Sorry," he says, holding up his hands. "I thought your mom *strongly disliked* Angelina after that whole ruining-her-life thing."

"Yeah, I know," Tara says. "I think coming here gives her some sort of closure. It brings her life full circle or something. Hey, look!" She points up to the top of one of the trees in front of the house. "It's Flo and Max! And they're not frozen!"

We all watch as the two hawks swoop down from the tree and land on the edge of the empty birdbath in the center of the yard. They start grooming each other as though they're yanked out of the normal stream of time every day.

"Did you bring them with us on purpose?" Connor asks me.

I shake my head. I don't want to tell him that I didn't want to bring any of *them* on purpose, either. If I did, I would have brought Bailey, too. She always has good ideas and I could use one right about now.

"Holy hamsters, Batman!" Bailey exclaims from somewhere behind me. "So this is the kind of thing you guys are always talking about!"

I whirl around so fast my neck hurts. There she is, standing beside the birdbath, holding what looks like a cup of lemonade with ice.

We all stare in shocked silence. Then Leo sticks out his finger and pokes her on the arm.

"Um, ouch?" she says, rubbing the spot.

Leo grins. "Yup, she's real."

"How did you get here?" I ask.

Bailey shakes her head. "Couldn't tell ya. One minute I was in study hall doodling my name on my sneaker" — she pauses to lift one leg up to show us her name in purple sparkly gel pen — "then the next I was here with you fine folks and this refreshing icy beverage." She lifts the glass in a toast. "Here's to freaky magic stuff!"

"It's my first time, too," David admits after she drains her cup. "I was starting to think all Grace could do was make pizza!"

Tara kicks him in the shin. "And cure your *dad*!" she says.

"Well, that, too," he admits, winking at me.

We all laugh, and for a second I almost forget why we're here. But only for a second. I bend down to look over the names of the herbs printed on tiny wooden sticks. I can't even pronounce half of them. "I wish Angelina had left a book of instructions," I mutter. Then I look up at the group hopefully.

They all shake their heads. I knew it was a long shot.

"Have you ever been inside Angelina's house?" Bailey asks me. "Maybe she *did* leave something for you."

"Amanda and I are pretty good at climbing in windows," Leo volunteers.

I get to my feet. "Knowing Angelina, she'd have a shark with its mouth open waiting under the window."

"No crime on my watch," Ray says. "I'm too pretty to go to jail."

Amanda and Tara roll their eyes.

"What if the key to the store isn't actually the key to the store?" Bailey asks. "What if you got it wrong and it's the key to the house?"

I hesitate. That would explain why I haven't been able to get into the shop. But then I shake my head. "I don't think so. Angelina's letter said the key would 'open doors to wonders unimagined,' and that Tara would know where to use it. So it's got to be the store."

"I agree," Tara says. "I've never been inside her house."

"We could still try it," Amanda says, stuffing what looks like a clump of blue flowers into her pocket. "If Angelina ever said exactly what she meant, I'd fall over in shock."

"Can't argue with that," Rory says. "It feels a little weird, though, to go in without permission."

Bailey pulls the pouch with the key out of her back pocket and holds it out to me.

I look at Tara. She shrugs. "Angelina moves in mysterious ways. If there's something in there that could help you, I think you should do it."

I look back to Rory. She hesitates, then nods.

"Okay, I'll try." I take the key from Bailey and slowly climb the porch steps. With each step, I feel the pull of the house getting stronger, as if I'm being tugged by some unseen rope. One more strong yank, and I'm suddenly standing right in front of the door. I turn around to look at the others and see MYSELF, still standing on the second step, frozen with one foot in the air.

The rest of Team Grace is frozen, too. How can we be frozen in time when we're already *out* of time? How can I be both here and there?

I really should stop asking questions I have no hope of knowing the answers to. I put my hand on the door, and it opens without me even using the key. Instead of the wooden floor and painted walls I would have expected to see in an old house, I find myself in a lush, tropical garden that smells of ripe grapefruit and the sea. A circle of stone benches surrounds the garden. In the distance I can see the beach and can just make out the sound of the surf lapping at the shoreline. It is the most beautiful and relaxing place I have ever been.

And I have been here before.

When I lay frozen in bed the week after my birthday, feeling the vortex's power run through my veins, I wasn't in the hospital, or in my bedroom. I was HERE. This garden paradise, this is the place that kept me safe, and sane. And I had forgotten all about it.

The benches are empty, except for one. I should be surprised to see her here, duck-shaped birthmark and all, but somehow I'm not.

"Are you real?" I ask Angelina.

She smoothes out the long brown dress she's wearing. "That depends. Quantum physics tells us reality is actually not real at all. What we think of as solid matter turns out to be invisible waves of energy existing in a field of mathematical possibilities. Once you choose a direction, only then does it become real."

"Um, that's a little beyond my fifth-grade science unit."

"Perhaps," she agrees. "But you will need to know this one day, so don't forget it."

I've already half forgotten it now! My bare feet sink a little deeper into the soft, white sand. "Where am I?" I ask. "Are we actually inside your house?"

She shakes her head. "You are nowhere, and you are everywhere."

I cross my arms. "Seriously? That's the answer you're going with? First quantum physics and now *nowhere and everywhere?*"

She chuckles. "We are in your power center, my feisty little friend, your higher self, if you will. You built this place with your imagination, but you breathed life into it, and now it's as real as anyplace else. When you're ready, this is where you will come to focus your power. For now, it waits."

"I'm ready," I tell her. "What's it waiting for?"

"For you to get stronger, young Grace. What is the rush to end your childhood? Ask your friend Rory how well that worked for her. The turning of the planet will march you inevitably forward either way. I've been alive more than a century and it still doesn't feel like enough."

It's not like I don't *want* to spend my days playing with Bailey, sewing funny outfits, and dancing really badly, but I am part of something much bigger than myself now, and no amount of ignoring that fact is going to change it.

She taps her foot, waiting for an answer. But I don't know how much to tell her about wanting to make my parents forget, or about the "big thing" that I want to be prepared for when it comes. Especially when I have no idea what that big thing is.

Meanwhile, Angelina reaches for a glass beside her. Ice cubes clink against the sides as she sips. Good thing my imaginary power center is polite enough to offer drinks to its guests!

"You surprise me, Grace," she says after emptying the glass. "You are already stronger than I thought you would be so soon after draining your power. You have your own secrets, as I had mine. Soon you will begin to see where your gifts are needed. It may happen differently for you than it did for me. Time will tell."

"I really am ready," I repeat.

"You may or may not be," she says, sounding a bit bored now. "There are many ways to connect to the source. Each will strengthen your connection to the power in a different way and will help you learn to control it. Experiment. Train yourself. Offer gratitude."

Okay, that's vague, but at least it sounds like a start. "So . . . um, how exactly am I supposed to do all that?"

She shakes her head at me. "Doesn't anyone go to the library anymore?"

Before I can argue that I was, in fact, just at the library last week to return the summer reading books Rory picked out for me, I am whisked out of the garden until I'm back inside my body, the key still unused in my hand. "Wait!" a voice shouts as I reach one hand out to the porch railing to steady myself. At first I think it's *my* voice calling out to Angelina. But Rory is the one shouting. I force myself to focus on being back in the front yard. The others are all moving around like normal again. They must not have noticed anything different while I was gone. Rory runs up the steps and grips my arm.

"*Wait*," she repeats. "I don't think the answer's inside. Look." She faces me toward Angelina's garden. At first I don't see anything different. But then Max swoops down low, grabs a clump of purple stalks in his beak, and drops them into the center of the birdbath. Flo approaches from the other side and adds a batch of green stems with tiny white flowers at the ends. Then they both fly off to different parts of the garden and do it all over again.

"You may not know how to make a forgetting potion," Rory says. "But they do."

AMANDA

Dear Diary,

So it wasn't even a full week before Grace pulled us out of time and brought us to Angelina's house. I'm not blaming her, but I'm not even really sure why she needed all of us there. I was trying to be normal for a change, sitting in biology class, learning about DNA and how the human genome has a blueprint for not only our bodies but also for all of life on the planet hidden inside it, when suddenly the plastic double helix that Mrs. Robinson was holding up stopped swaying in midair.

"Sweet!" Leo said from his stool next to me. He waved his hand in front of the faces of the two kids sitting across from us at the lab table. "Guess we have Grace to thank for this break from learning!"

Biology and lunch are the only times I see Leo during the day. When it was time to choose lab partners, none of the other kids even glanced our way, like they wouldn't have even considered asking either of us. So we chose each other. We've been choosing each other since the day we were born. But actually, when you think about it, we didn't really have a choice at all. It wasn't like we were waiting up in heaven — or wherever you wait before you're born, if there is such a place — and said, let's be born on the same day! And be best friends! And later, girlfriend and boyfriend!

At least I'm pretty sure we didn't. I sound like I'm complaining. I don't mean to. I don't think I mean to. When I was eleven, Kylie told me being thirteen is hard! She was SOOOO right. I never thought I'd miss being younger, and I definitely like the independence of thirteen, but I could do without feeling like sometimes I don't know myself anymore. Like Stephanie's pool party. It was okay, and her friends were nice to me and all. But I wish it had been just the two of us. Sometimes I would catch her eye across the pool and know she was thinking the same thing. I don't really talk to her about Leo even when we ARE alone. When one person has a boyfriend and the other doesn't, it just comes out sounding obnoxious when you complain about yours.

Anyway, so after everyone turned all statue-like, Leo hopped off his stool and shouted something like, "The adventure begins!" But all I said was, "Didn't Grace say she wouldn't need us for a while?"

And Leo said, "I guess she said that. But you know how these things go."

And, Diary, let me tell ya, I DO know how these things go. I told Leo to go ahead and I would meet him.

"Okay," he said. He hesitated, though, and I knew he didn't want to leave me behind, so I said, "Hey, maybe there'll be pizza." He squeezed my hand and ran out. As soon as he left the room, I took out the folded piece of paper I've carried in my back pocket for a week. I've read the phone number over and over. I still haven't called it, yet. I tucked it back away and then ran out to join the others.

At Angelina's house, Leo kept looking at me, and I know he was wondering if everything was okay, but he didn't ask, which I'm glad about. I was also glad when Grace wound up not going inside. It just felt wrong. I don't know when Angelina is going to be home, but entering her house without asking felt like invading her privacy. I think the key is for the store, anyway.

So then, Diary, things took a weird turn (as though all the rest wasn't weird enough!!! But that's my life, I guess, measuring things in weird, weirder, weirder still, and weirdEST). Anyway, we got back to school and Grace told us to count to a hundred before she started time up again. That way we'd all have a chance to get back where we were before it happened, and no one around us would notice anything. David had to go back to the bathroom and lock himself in a stall, which was kind of funny.

So Leo and I got back to biology class, and something about the way he looked at me as we climbed up onto our stools made me feel a little dizzy and warm. I glanced quickly around the room to make sure everyone was still frozen. Leo was counting out loud. "Seventy-eight . . . seventy-nine . . . eighty . . ."

Before he could say eighty-one, I leaned over and pressed my cheek against his cheek. I closed my eyes. He wound his fingers through my hair and the dizzy feeling grew. We stayed like that, him breathing the numbers out into my ear, me just breathing.

"Ninety-eight . . . ninety-nine . . ."

I pulled away and we both turned to face Mrs. Robinson, who continued telling the class about the miracle of life.

RORY

RORY: see pic below!!!!

ANNABELLE: You're going to make yourself crazy if you believe everything you read about him. There's not even a picture.

I know, I know, but I texted him this morning to see if it was true, and he didn't answer.

It's the middle of the night there. Plus, if that article is true, which I'm sure it's not, then he might still be out dancing!!

Bleh. :(

Honestly I'm not sure mere mortals are supposed to be in a relationship with movie stars.

I know, it's crazy-making. Hold on, doorbell. Probably paperboy wanting to be paid.

What's a paperboy?

Been 5 mins. Forget about me?

Roooooryyyyy. Helllloooooo?

I'm just going to start singing until you come back. Lalalala, this is my song. Doh Re Mi Fa So La Ti Doh. Ti Doh! Tea Dough! Tito! OMG I think I'm losing my mind. Twenty minutes now.

SOOOOOO sorry!

Finally! Paperboy? Whatever that is?

No . . . guess again.

Sunshine Kid selling cookies? Early trick-or-treater?

Nope.

I give up.

HEY, ANNABELLE, THIS IS JAKE. HOW ARE YA?

Er, um, huh? What?

CAME TO SURPRISE RORY. SURPRISE!

Uh . . . aren't you in Hollywood right now? You know, dancing up a storm with uberwitch Madison? I mean, that lovely girl, Madison?

ONLY IF HOLLYWOOD IS IN WILLOW FALLS THESE DAYS. AND

JUDGING BY THE LACK OF TAN SKIN AND FAKE BLOND HAIR, I'M GONNA SAY IT'S NOT.

But there's no way you could have gotten here so fast after the show and the dancing.

THEY FILM THOSE SHOWS IN THE AFTERNOON, THEN AIR THEM LATER. AND IT WASN'T ME WITH MADISON. IT'S MY NEW LOOK-ALIKE, A KID NAMED CARSON! NOW I CAN BE IN TWO PLACES AT ONCE. VOILÀ! MAGIC!

Okay then. You know it's a school day, though, right? Did you miss our school so much you felt the overwhelming urge to come back?

LOL. YOUR SCHOOL IS NOT WITHOUT ITS CHARMS, BUT NO. HERE'S RORY.

Okay, it's me again. My parents said we can skip school today. Sawyer is losing-his-mind excited. We're all going hiking at the reservoir.

Have fun. Try not to fall into the water.

I'll do my best. XOX

LEO

Ode to Our Compost Heap (Part One)
By Leo Fitzpatrick

O compost heap, you are so smelly
Full of worms and dung and bones and jelly.
But we're doing our part to save the world
Or so I'm told.

The thing that I like most about you,
Is the time I spend thinking while shoveling your goo.

I don't only think about eating, you know,
Even though most people would think so.

My head is full of other stuff,
Like sometimes with Amanda things get tough.

A teenage girl must be a hard thing to be,
They worry about things that are foreign to me.
I prefer to keep life simple,
(Although I really could do without this pimple!)

Ode to Our Compost Heap (Part Two)

Washing off the sweat and dirt
Always puts me in a happy mood.
Life is simpler when you work the earth
By turning garbage into plant food.

I will bring some compost up to Apple Grove
For our little trees struggling to take hold.
I've never told Amanda this (in case she doesn't feel
   the same)
But those trees are a part of us,
And I've given each a name.
Bert and Hortense and Morris and Sue
Mac and Ann and Phil.

Okay, so those last lines don't rhyme,
But, really, that's no crime,
Because yesterday I got pulled from time.

And if time had stopped forever
During those last ten seconds,
With my hand in her hair
And her breath in my ear
I wouldn't have minded a bit.

TARA

Dear Julie,

My dad and I drove all the way home (to our old home) to arrange for the moving people. The house sold in less than a week! Apparently the people who bought it are huge fans of my dad and simply HAD to own the house where *My Mailman Was the Leader of the Alien Zombie Apocalypse* was written. My dad said now that I'm thirteen, I can start reading his books. I'm not sure I want to, though. What if I don't like them? That would make for some awkward dinner table conversation! :0) Maybe YOU can read them?

w/b/s

Tara

PS: About David . . . he makes me a nicer person. How's that for mushy?? I haven't seen him as much as I thought I would, but he's been really busy with his dad and I've been busy moving . . . so, you know. It's okay, though. Not every couple can be glued at the hip like Amanda and Leo.

Chapter Five

GRACE

The thing about making a forgetting spell is that I have no idea how to do it. Sure, the hawks gave me the ingredients, but being able to understand the language of birds must not be in my job description. And don't think I didn't try, because I did. I asked them what I should do with the herbs and flowers they gave me, but they just made this loud *kreeee* sound (which was like the bird equivalent of rolling their eyes) and flew off.

Tara offered to ask her mom if she knew anything about preparing potions. After all, it was a potion from Angelina that indirectly led to their family moving here. Plus, her mom knows a lot about gardens and herbs. Mrs. Brennan was happy to help, so now I have a whole list of instructions.

"Ready?" Bailey asks, rolling up her sleeves. She's come over to help me prepare the potion. The first step was to dry out the herbs and flowers, so they've been hanging upside down in small bundles in my closet for a week. I was afraid Mom would find them when she put away my clothes, but she's been so distracted lately I don't think she's done laundry all week. Or maybe all month. I'm down to one clean sock.

When I unclip the herbs from the hanger, a few stiff, white petals fall to the floor. I can't take any chances on messing up the recipe, so I crawl around the closet and pick them out of the carpet.

Suddenly a low, rumbly voice reaches my ears. I duck my head out of the closet. "Did you say something?" I ask Bailey.

She shakes her head.

I crawl back in to get the last leaf and hear it again. A man's voice for sure. "Just give me one more chance," he says. "I won't let you down."

"Bailey!" I call out in a loud whisper. "I think someone is trying to reach out to me! I'm hearing voices!"

"So am I," she whispers back.

My eyes widen. "You are? Maybe you share my powers because you're my best friend!"

"Pretty sure that's not it," she says, pointing to the back of the closet. "It's coming from in there."

We push past the hanging clothes and press our ears up to the back wall. Sure enough, the voice comes through again.

"One more day, Mr. Murphy, you'll see. Things at home have been" — he pauses and I picture him stopping to gulp down what's probably his tenth coffee of the day — "difficult," he finishes.

"Mr. Murphy is my dad's boss," I whisper, my heart thumping.

"I thought your dad was still at work," Bailey whispers back.

"So did I." We wait for another minute, but my dad must have gotten off the phone or moved farther away from his bedroom wall. I grab Bailey's sleeve and tug her through the clothes again.

"That didn't sound good," she says once we've closed the closet door behind us. "It sounds like he might get fired!"

I don't answer. I have a tight ball in the pit of my stomach. I stuff the crumbly herbs into the bowl I'd snagged from the kitchen earlier. "Let's hurry up with this. Looks like we don't have any time to waste. We have to save my dad's job!"

Half an hour later we've ground the herbs into a fine powder using a rock and a bowl, soaked them in vinegar, strained them with my last remaining sock, and are in the process of drying them in my Easy-Bake Oven. We could dry them in the microwave, but I don't want to risk running into a parent. Plus the Easy-Bake Oven still smells like the chocolate chip cookie Bailey and I made in there when we were seven. Before the vortex, baking that cookie in my toy oven was the most magical thing that had happened to me. Well, that and meeting Jake Harrison!

Connor's voice floats in from the hall. "It's me," he says, knocking on the door. "Can I come in?"

He never used to knock. I kind of wish he hadn't started treating me differently, but I can't blame him. My parents are obviously taking it the hardest, but having a sister in my situation can't be easy on him. I open the door and yank him inside.

He wrinkles his nose. "Why does it smell like Easter eggs in here?"

Bailey holds up the jar of vinegar.

"We're making the forgetting potion," I explain.

He bends down to peer inside the toy oven. "You know

that's just a one-hundred-watt lightbulb in there, right? It's not actually cooking anything?"

"We totally baked a cookie in there once," Bailey says, jutting out her lip.

"No, you didn't," he says. "I switched it out with a store-bought one when you guys weren't looking."

I put my hand over my ears. "I'm going to pretend I didn't hear that."

He picks up the list of instructions. "Why do you need to dry them twice if you're making tea? Won't they just get wet again?"

I glance over at the list. There does seem to be a lot of drying and wetting and drying again going on.

Connor whips out his phone. "I'll call Tara and ask." A few seconds later, he says, "Yo, New Girl! What's with this potion recipe you gave my lil sis? Is it legit?" He pauses to listen for a minute. "Okay, roger that." He slips the phone in his pocket and looks over to me. "Yeah, her mom may have guessed on a few steps."

I frown at the soggy mess inside the oven.

"Maybe you can just put it in the tea now," he suggests. "That should be fine, right?"

I shake my head slowly, not taking my eyes off the oven. A vision is unfolding in front of my eyes of me using the mixture. A brief snapshot, but it's enough. "I'm not putting it into tea after all," I tell them confidently.

"But, Grace," Bailey says. "You heard your dad. He could lose his job, your mom's a mess, and everyone's always bugging you at school about the hospital and whispering about how you grew four inches in one summer and —"

I look up in surprise. "I didn't think anyone at school noticed that."

"Trust me," she says. "Everyone noticed. You really need to —"

"Wait a second," Connor interrupts. "You heard Dad say he might lose his *job*?"

I nod. "Sorry I didn't tell you right away. I didn't want to worry you."

"It's not your job to protect me all the time," Connor says. It's the closest he's come to snapping at me since all this started. It kind of *is* my job to protect him, but I'm smart enough not to point that out. Instead I say calmly, "Anyway, I didn't mean I'm not going to do the spell, only that no one needs to drink it. Turns out it isn't for our parents, it's for me."

Connor and Bailey exchange their *Grace has lost it again* look. "What do you mean, for you?" Bailey asks. "Are you going to try to make *yourself* forget?"

I shake my head. "I just had a vision of me asleep with the herbs under my pillow."

"A vision?" Connor asks. "What do you mean?"

How can I explain? Maybe I shouldn't have said anything. I'm never sure what to tell and what to keep. I don't want to freak them out, or the other extreme — make them jealous — so I wind up keeping a lot from them. I still haven't told anyone about seeing Angelina in that garden at her house. That didn't feel like a vision, though, not in the way that this did. That felt like I was really in the garden with her.

"A vision is when a picture pops into my head," I explain. "Like, I'll see a scene that hasn't happened yet, or I'll see some place different from where I am."

"Does this happen a lot?" Connor asks, his voice thick with concern.

I shake my head. I won't ask his definition of *a lot*.

"That's good," he says. "I'm sure that'd be real distracting."

To change the subject, I ask Bailey if she has the pouch with the key in it.

She reaches into her backpack and roots around for it. "You're trying to get in the store again?" she asks, handing me the pouch.

"Not yet," I reply as I pull out the key and tuck it into my desk drawer. "I think I'll know when it's time to go back there." I open the oven door and slide out the little tray. The mixture is only a little drier than when we stuck it in there. I place my hands over the tray and focus on pushing warmth out through my palms. In seconds, the mixture is dry again. I let my hands fall to my sides.

Connor breathes in sharply. "Wow, how did you do that?"

"I don't know," I admit. "I just suddenly knew I could." Before they can ask anything else that I won't know the answer to, I grab the pouch and pour the dried herbs into it. Then I head over to the bed and stuff the pouch under my pillow. Tonight's the night.

· · · · · · · · · · · · ·

Dinner is very quiet. Mom and Dad basically push food around their plates the whole time. Dad is wearing sweatpants instead of his business suit. It's like he's given up already. I don't have to be a mind reader to know Connor and I are thinking the same thing — this spell better work!

Connor comes into the bathroom later while I'm brushing my teeth. "Are you ready?" he asks. "Did your vision thingy show you what's going to happen?"

I shake my head and spit into the sink. "All I saw was me sleeping with the pouch under my pillow."

"Did it show you with your mouth open and drooling?"

I punch him in the arm. He doesn't seem fazed.

"I know!" he says, backing away. "It showed you snoring and talking in your sleep, right?"

I wait until his mouth is full of toothpaste. "Keep it up, big brother. Maybe I'll add to the forgetting spell that you forget how to tie your shoes."

He tries to answer, but I run out before he gets the chance. I don't really mind him teasing me (even though I do *not* drool in my sleep!). Teasing is still better than him treating me like a fragile creature that's going to break any second.

I climb into bed, and once I get used to my head being higher on my pillow than usual, I relax pretty quickly. With my eyes closed, I try to clear my mind of all the worries of the day (there were a lot!). After a few minutes I start thinking about my garden, and how Angelina said that's where my power is waiting for me. But how do I get back there? I've tried imagining myself walking into Angelina's house again, but each time I do, I just see a regular house. No tropical garden in sight. When I had visited the garden while I was in the coma, I hadn't made any specific effort to get there, I was just *there*.

Maybe I'm making it too complicated. Angelina said the garden was my higher self. What *is* a higher self? It's got to be higher than my regular self, right? Okay, so what are some ways to go up? An airplane? A staircase? Before I know it, I'm picturing myself stepping into an elevator. It's carpeted, with gleaming mahogany walls. Like a regular elevator, there are buttons to press for each floor. Only these don't have numbers on them. *Not helpful, imagination!*

I take a chance and press the top button. Speakers pipe out light jazz music as the elevator rises. I find myself tapping my foot along to the beat. After what feels like a long time, a bell dings. The doors slide open to reveal a whiteness so blinding, so utterly all encompassing, that for a second I forget where I am and who I am. All is completely quiet, and yet it's the loudest place I've ever been. Or at least I *think* it is, since I have no memory of being anywhere other than here. Then the doors automatically swoosh closed, and the walls, floor, and ceiling of the elevator reappear. I blink and take a breath. I may have gone a bit too high.

Chapter Six

GRACE

With a shaking finger, I press the middle button.

The elevator descends slowly. *Ding*. Then, *swoosh*. The fresh breeze reaches me first, followed by the smell of flowers and ocean air. My garden! I hurry out before the doors can close again. The stone benches are gone, and in their place are a row of beach chairs. Three tropical birds with long orange feathers have taken up residence in the nearby palm trees. I reach out and an icy lemonade appears in my hand. I take a sip. *Ahhh*, refreshing! I could get used to this.

I wander around the garden, feeling the sand and soft grass beneath my feet. In the same way that I knew how to dry out the herbs with my hands, I know that every single person has a place like this inside them. Most people will never find it because they don't even know to look for it. I could hang here all day, just exploring.

But I'm not here on vacation — I have a mission. Reluctantly I give a pat on the head to the fluffy, orange kitten that has appeared in my arms and lay him down on a patch of clovers. Then I walk over to the beach and look around my feet until I find a stick with a pointy end.

The tide has just gone out, leaving a swath of wet sand along the shoreline. I think about all the people who love me and who are rooting for me, and imagine a bubble of light surrounding each of them, protecting them, keeping them safe.

I let my mind wander back to the moment my parents brought me to the hospital on my birthday. I had just been hit with all my powers and I was slipping away. I knew where they were taking me, and I knew they were so scared, but I had no way of telling them they shouldn't worry. Their joy when I awoke quickly turned to fear and worry when they learned about my powers and how much responsibility was now on my shoulders. I know they were happy I had been able to help cure David's father, but they weren't shy about letting me know they wished the vortex had chosen someone else's daughter. I can't give them that, but maybe I can give them this.

I hold the stick like a giant pencil, and in my best handwriting, I write the word *FORGET.* As I craft each letter, I imagine myself pulling the memories of the last two months from my parents' heads, like a spool of thread unraveling. Then I stitch the gaps together so they don't feel the loss of time.

Once the word is complete, I lie down on the sand next to it and close my eyes. When I open them again, I'm in my bedroom like I never left. Which, I guess, I didn't.

It's still dark, and my alarm clock reveals it's not yet midnight. My door flies open, and I sit upright. The light on in the hall reveals the shape of Connor standing in my doorway in his pajamas with the Minecraft characters all over them. Maybe the knocking-before-entering thing wasn't so bad!

"What is it?" I ask him, squinting.

"You have to see this!" he says. "Come on!"

I hurry out of bed and follow him down the hall. "What is it?" I ask. "Is everything okay?"

He waves for me to follow him down the stairs and then stops halfway, just far enough to let us peek into the living room below. "Look!"

One of Dad's favorite classic rock songs is playing from the portable speaker on the coffee table. I haven't heard music in the house in two months. That in itself would be a good sign that the spell worked. But what seals the deal is the fact that my parents are dancing! In their pajamas! Around the living room!

"You did it!" Connor says, squeezing my arm.

"Let's go back up," I reply. "I think they want to be alone."

We giggle like when we were little kids, and sneak back up the stairs. We run back into my room and have just shut the door behind us when my cell phone starts ringing.

"Do you have some big secret life I don't know about?" Connor jokes. "Who would be calling you at midnight?"

"I have no idea," I reply. "But I'm pretty sure I only have one secret life."

I grab my phone from the dresser and turn it over to see the caller's name. "It's David!" I tell Connor as I press the speakerphone button. At the same time Connor and I ask, "Is everything okay?" David starts talking so fast I can barely make out his words. I think he's crying, too.

"Slow down," I ask. "I don't understand. Your grandfather what?"

"There's a picture of my grandfather on my night table!" he shouts.

"Um, that's good that you're close?" I reply, not sure what to say.

"No, you don't understand," he cries. "My grandfather died when my father was three years old! I never met him! But now he's alive and living in Florida, and I went to the zoo with him and we pet a giraffe! It's in the photograph!"

What he's saying finally sinks in. Connor must have gotten it at the same time because he inhales sharply and sits down on the bed.

"And that's not all!" David says. "All the piles of paperwork and news articles and old medicines of my dad's, they're all gone! Like they never existed! The house is filled with other stuff that was never here — games and books and sports stuff and a huge family tree on the wall going back to the founding of Willow Falls! Did you know it was originally going to be called Willow Hills? Anyway, we never moved away after my great-great-grandfather got sick because he NEVER GOT SICK! It looks like that forgetting potion not only made all the doctors forget about my dad, it made the disease forget about itself! You did that, Grace!" He's full-on crying now. "You saved my whole family!"

I'm so speechless that I just let the phone fall to the carpet. Connor swoops it up. "Hold on, buddy," he says to David before turning to me. "Are you going to be okay, lil sis, savior of a long line of Goldberg men? Why don't you get back in bed."

I let him lead me back to my bed and help me climb in. I curl up around Green Bunny, my bedtime companion since I was four. Connor pats me and then the bunny on the head. "You did good," he whispers, then takes the phone with him and shuts the door.

My head is spinning. When I made my parents forget about me having special powers, that meant they had to forget about me healing David's dad! And I guess by doing that, they had to forget he was ever sick. Like a stack of dominoes falling over, one event undid another until the first person in David's family to get the disease — his great-great-grandfather — never got it! Tears start to slide out of the sides of my eyes — a mixture of relief, gratitude, and amazement, along with a little bit of fear at the power I seem to be able to wield.

After a few minutes, it occurs to me that I can't feel the lump of herbs under my pillow anymore. I sit up, turn on the lamp, and lift the pillow. The pouch is still there, but it's flat. I unzip it and peer inside. The herbs are completely gone. Not even one ground-up flower wedged in a corner. What is there, however, is a postcard. I pull it out. Instead of the huge rocks of Stonehenge on the front, three giant stone pyramids stare up at me along with the words, *Greetings from . . . the Great Pyramids of Egypt!*

I flip it over to find only one sentence scribbled on the back in Angelina's unmistakable handwriting:

The student has surpassed the teacher.

I peer closer. On the very bottom are two more words in letters so small I have to hold the postcard up to the lamp to read them.

Thank you.

I trace the final words with my fingers. I know why she's thanking me. She can finally let go of the guilt of not being able to cure David's great-great-grandfather. I am grateful that I can give that to her, but I can't help worrying, too. Who am I to play with people's lives in this way? I'm thrilled for the Goldbergs of course, but what about all the other people I *didn't* help?

I keep dwelling on this question as my hand slides over the letters. "Ouch!" I yelp, yanking my hand away. It felt like a little spark jumped off the paper and into my finger. I look back down at the card, expecting to see a scorch mark. Instead, there are new words where the large blank space used to be!

Young Grace, these questions are too big for you to ask. The vortex chose us for reasons that are its own. Perhaps we will know them one day, or perhaps not. Until then, trust.

I touch my fingers gently to the words. I don't get a shock this time. "I'll try," I whisper. "Good night, Angelina."

But the postcard stays silent.

AMANDA

Dear Diary,

I have a lot to catch you up on. Good and not so good. First, whenever I see David at school he's grinning so wide his cheeks must hurt. He showed all of us his big family tree on his wall and it's AMAZING. I see his parents around town and everyone treats them like they've always been here. It's SOOOO weird!!! But very cool!!

On the Team Grace front, we've been pretty much all doing our own thing. Grace has been lying low since her forgetting spell worked so well. She and Bailey have been off doing normal kid stuff, which is really great. I ran into them at the Willow Falls Diner eating chocolate chip pancakes and they had chocolate all over them and they didn't even mind. That's what it's like at their age. I remember when I didn't care, and it wasn't even so long ago. Tara and Rory cornered me in the cafeteria last week and asked me if everything was okay because I've been kind of quiet lately, and I said that everything's fine, but I'm not so sure it is.

Something happened today that I feel really weird about. That's the "not so good" thing I said was coming. A week or two after school started, I saw this flyer at the music store when I stopped in to get new drumsticks. The flyer said some kids from the high school were forming a band and needed a drummer. You know how I'm good friends with the owners of the store — Larry and Laurence? Remember how they always said one day I'd be old enough to be in a real band? I guess since you're a diary and not a real person you wouldn't know that, but trust me, they did say that. Still, I wasn't really going to do it because between homework and Leo and Team Grace and marching band, I don't really have time even if I DID get in, which I probably wouldn't. Anyway, then Kylie saw the flyer on my desk. I thought she was going to tell me I was crazy and that I'd never make it. But she told me that even though she didn't really get how banging the drums was music, other people seemed to think I had talent, and hadn't I always said I wanted to be in a band that didn't march?

Leo texted me while I was riding my bike over to the audition, but I didn't answer. I didn't want to lie and make up some reason why I wasn't home. I just wanted this to be mine.

The downstairs room of the music store was full of people practicing on invisible drums while they waited their turn. There were some other girls, but I was the youngest by a few years.

I'll cut to the chase, Diary. I didn't make the band. But as I was leaving, this guy in Kylie's grade asked if I wanted to get coffee and talk about playing the drums. I don't "get coffee" because ICK, it's so gross, and also Rory once drank way too much and went, like, totally bonkers, and we should really learn from the mistakes of our friends.

But did I mention the guy was really cute and boys don't ask me out? And it's not because they know about Leo, it's because they just don't. Or haven't before this, anyway.

Also, I heard Kylie's voice in my head telling me I should go because she always says you never know if the perfect guy for you is just around the corner, and I know she thinks I'm with Leo just because he's "comfortable." So I said okay to the guy whose name was Christian or Tristan or Justin (it was loud in the music store when he first told me his name). We went down the street to the Friendly

Bean, a coffee shop in town that the high school kids go to, but where I've never been.

We both got iced teas, and he made some joke about how he should have invited me for tea instead of coffee but then we'd sound like little old ladies. I laughed. That joke was the high point of the date because, Diary, I swear, not five minutes after we sat down, LEO'S MOTHER WALKS IN and orders a coffee! Darn this small town!!

She saw me at the exact second I saw her, so there was no chance of ducking. I'd describe her first reaction as surprised and happy to see me, then her second one as just surprise, then her third as confusion, then her fourth as embarrassment. I would describe mine as: horror, followed by more horror, and then even more horror.

She gave me a little wave and left without even getting her coffee. Christian/Tristan/Justin was talking about this new snare drum he's saving up to buy at the music store, but my head was buzzing and I couldn't hear him.

When I got home from the date or whatever it was, I told Kylie what happened and I thought she was going to say I was stupid for even worrying about it since I'm my own person and Leo is Leo and he'll always be there, but instead she threw a pillow at me and yelled, "What is wrong with you? You have a perfectly good boyfriend and you risk messing it up?"

Well, Diary, my mouth fell open on that one! When I tried to argue that she was the one who said I shouldn't let Leo hold me back, she said, "Don't listen to ME! I've never had someone love me since I was born like you have! I mean, except for family of course and that doesn't count!"

I tried to argue that of course family counts, but I knew that wasn't really her point.

"It was just coffee," I argue.

Then she says, "How would you feel if Leo didn't reply to your text and then went out for 'just coffee' with some random girl?"

Feeling defiant, I crossed my arms and said, "I wouldn't care. He's his own person and we're only thirteen. We have our whole lives ahead of us."

"That's right," she said. "And you can either have it with someone you love and who loves you even when you're a pain in the butt, which you've been lately, or you can spend it trying to replace that person. Your choice."

She's right. I know she's right. So of course I stormed out of her room and that's why I'm writing this to you.

Maybe Mrs. Fitzpatrick didn't tell Leo she saw me. That's possible, right?

LEO

Heartbreak & Despair
By Leo Fitzpatrick

She doesn't even *like* coffee.

I admit it — my heart does kinda ache,
It actually feels like it's going to break.
I've been here before,
But I guess I'm back for more.

Why was she with some other guy?
I've got to man up, I can't start to cry.
I know three years ago I hurt her really bad,
I hope she didn't feel half this sad.

She's my best friend,
And I'll stand by her to the end.
I just want her to be happy,
Even if it makes me feel crappy.

I hope the guy had bad breath.

RORY

ANNABELLE: Don't freak out.

RORY: How can I not freak out if you start a text with "don't freak out"?

Just do your best. And remember, it doesn't mean anything.

Just tell me!

Remember a few weeks ago when Jake surprised you and then your family brought him hiking down near the reservoir and you fell and he had to carry you out?

I didn't fall! I was just showing him the drainpipe I got stuck in that one time. And then, okay, I sort of fell. What about it?

Wait, you were stuck in a drainpipe?

Moving on . . . so what am I not supposed to freak out about?

This.

Whoa! Where did that picture of me and Jake come from? My parents were there, but they were in the visitors' center when that happened! We were totally alone!

Well, someone else must have been there. It goes with this article from *Teen Scene Today* **. . .**

Jake's Mystery Girl!

By I. M. Sneaky Pete

Here at *Teen Scene Today* we've been holding onto this juicy picture until we found out the mystery girl's identity. And thanks to none other than Jake's GF, Madison Waters, we finally have! In an exclusive interview Madison said this: "Yeah, I know her. She's that poor, sad girl who was always following my Jake around the set when we were filming in that sad little town. She kept falling down or swelling up. She was a mess. Jake took pity on her." So there you have it, folks!

You okay?

Ror?

Um, Rory?

I'm on my way.

DAVID

To: Linda@OnlineFamilyTherapy.com
From: DavidGoldberg@WillowFallsSchool.edu
Subject: Checking in
Hello, my name is David Goldberg. You sent me a new patient questionnaire a while ago, and I'm still waiting to hear your response. Can you let me know when you'll be writing back? Thanks.

From: Linda@OnlineFamilyTherapy.com
To: DavidGoldberg@WillowFallsSchool.edu
Subject: Re: Checking in
Dear David,
We are very sorry for any confusion, but we have no record of you as a patient. Perhaps you signed up with a

different online therapy program? If you are in need of our services, we are happy to help. Otherwise, best of luck to you.

Sincerely,

Linda, Online Family Therapist

Dear Linda,

May I call you that? I'm not actually going to press SEND on this email anyway, so I guess it doesn't really matter. I could call you Linda, or Lin, or Linny-loo, and you'd never know it! Haha I crack myself up. :O) I figured out why you have no record of me. It was wiped out thanks to my friend Grace. More on her in a minute.

So, Linda, you'll never guess what I've been doing since my last email (even though YOU don't remember me filling out that questionnaire, I still remember). I've been very busy. After school I've been delivering meals to old people. And feeding meters on Main Street. Last weekend I sang songs on the street corner to raise money for Dog Adoption Day at the animal shelter. And I'm allergic to dogs! (You should consider adding allergies to your initial questionnaire.)

Basically, Linda, I'm doing my best to pay it forward. I'm trying to deserve the bounty of blessings that has come my way. You see, it was one thing when Grace and

Angelina cured my dad of his disease (yes, it's magic — how 'bout that?!! — that's another thing I can't tell you about of course, but again, not hitting SEND!), but then to free him of the burden of KNOWING he'd been miraculously cured? What a truly astonishing gift! And I don't throw a word like astonishing around lightly! What thirteen-year-old boy does? But that's what it is! Until I saw my father that first morning after Grace's forgetting spell, I hadn't realized how hard his sudden recovery had been for him, and how much he was covering that up for my sake. But that happy-to-be-alive glint was back in his eye, and a calmness that I hadn't seen all summer had settled on his face.

When I was little and asked my mom why she took so many pictures and videos of me, she said parents are the keepers of their children's memories until they're old enough to hold their own. I'm the keeper of my family's memories now. I'm the only one who knows the real version of events.

At first, the hardest part of adjusting to this "new normal" was losing the bond my mother and I had formed. For the last five years it's been the two of us against the world. Now she won't remember it.

On the other hand, I now have all these memories of life as a family that I never had before. Trips to visit grandparents, seeing Dad at all those school concerts and ball games that he'd missed, laughter around the dinner table, Dad helping me practice for my bar mitzvah. That's definitely the biggest change. At least my friends still remember me practicing in the empty pool hole across the street. If my friends had forgotten everything we'd been through together, I probably would have lost my mind.

Tara has been my rock. She gave me my favorite bar mitzvah gift — shards of colored glass around a picture frame. It's supposed to represent the ancient idea of *Tikkun Olam*, how each of us can do our part to repair the world. I look at it now and I see something I didn't before. When I stand back, the surface of the pieces reflect the world around me like a solid mirror. But I can also see myself in each of the tiny, broken fragments. Recent events lead me to believe that the world is like that, too — people are the individual fragments, but we are also part of the whole mirror. We are connected, not only to one another but also to the fabric of the universe. Grace can see these invisible bonds, and somehow she can rearrange the pieces. I am so grateful she arranged them in my favor. I will continue to repair the world in her honor.

Thanks for listening, Linda! You were really helpful, even though you'll never know it!

May the force be with you. Live long and prosper. (Mixing *Star Wars* and *Star Trek* there. Connor would turn green and keel over!)

Till we meet again,
David Goldberg

CONNOR

CONNOR KELLY'S INVENTOR'S JOURNAL
Type of product: 3-D Screen
Inventor: Connor Kelly
Description of invention-in-progress: My mentor, Roger St. Claire, told me to follow my passions when it comes to what to invent. My passion is video games. Not just because they're fun and challenging, but because I enjoy entering another world that someone else dreamed up. It's not like I'm addicted or anything, no matter what my mom might mutter under her breath when she'd rather I be doing homework. Anyway, it seems to me the end goal for a gamer like myself is to feel fully immersed in that other world. And for that, we need three-dimensional virtual

reality. Since I am not a computer programmer, and there's no way I would be able to build an actual VR device, I am going to follow another of my mentor's bits of wisdom. He said that an inventor doesn't need to invent the entire product, that sometimes inventing one piece of the puzzle can bring more success because that one piece might be useful in lots of different products. (He put it better than that, but that's the gist of it.) So then I thought, Why can't someone invent a screen that would fit over your computer or TV or phone or tablet or even a whole movie screen that would project the content in 3-D *without* glasses?

What problem does it solve: While it wouldn't be the virtual reality of my dreams, this product would save people the cost of having to buy 3-D glasses and would make it possible to view 3-D content wherever they are, without having to worry about having glasses with them.

Who will want or need this product: All fans of 3-D movies (which is of course everyone).

Materials: polarizing filters, organic polymer, calcium carbonate crystals, knowledge of 3-D tech

Steps: Analyze existing 3-D glasses to see how we can create filter for TV from them.

Results: Fingers crossed at this point!

Final observations: I'll tell ya when it's done!

Personal note: Even though my invention must remain a secret even to those closest to me (inventors are like magicians that way — can't reveal our tricks!), I am grateful that right now my life is back to normal enough that I can do this. Thanks, Grace! You've got skills, girl!

Chapter Seven

GRACE

Most kids might not think that riding the bus to school is all that awesomesauce, but that's only until your mom makes you go with her every morning and then lectures you about not using your magical powers the whole way to school and then picks you up and lectures you the whole way home. But now I'm back on the bus, baby! Woo-hoo! Bailey gets on soon, and all is right with the world!

All doubts about whether I did the right thing with the forgetting spell went away by the end of the first day. The difference in my parents' behavior is shocking. I knew it was bad, but now that they're back to normal, I can see how awful it had actually gotten. Our house feels like a home again, with yummy home-cooked food smells instead of takeout. Dad is back to blasting his old classic rock songs, which Connor and I used to complain about but are now a hugely welcome change from the awkward silences. Dad's quickly putting the weight back on that he'd lost, and our backyard vegetable garden is flourishing.

Without the added strain from our parents' constant worrying, Connor has returned to his inventions with a new spring in his step. I'm curious what he's working on but am doing my best not to be nosy and peek in the Inventor's Journal that Tara's uncle gave him.

I've been surprised how quickly my own life went back to how it was before Angelina and the vortex entered it. I can actually LEARN stuff at school without everyone making a fuss over me. I can walk through the halls without any second glances. Once a day or so, a kid will comment on my summer growth spurt, but that's not a bad thing. And Mom and I are busy doing what we always did — we make up silly songs together, shop, bake, and she helps me with my homework. I've hidden Angelina's two postcards (along with the instructions on brewing the forgetting spell and the key to the store) in the pouch. Then I hid the pouch in my bottom desk drawer.

I haven't even been tempted to try the key lately. I know I still need to get to the library like Angelina told me to so I can start learning how to work with my powers, but it's kind of nice being normal again. Or I guess I should say *pretending* to be normal, because I know I'm living on borrowed time.

I look out the bus window as it pulls up to Bailey's stop. Suddenly a vision flashes through my head. My shoulders sag as I realize I'll be leaving "normal" behind sooner than I'd expected.

"Yo," Bailey says, plopping down on the seat next to me. "Why the serious face? You don't want it to freeze that way." She laughs at her own joke.

I force a smile.

"Better," she says, tucking her backpack under our seat.

"Time's up," I say softly.

"What do you mean?"

I point out the window at a woman walking her dog on the sidewalk.

"So?" Bailey asks. "Do you know her?"

I shake my head. On the other side of the street, a squirrel scampers down a tree with a pinecone in its mouth. A second later, the dog breaks free from its leash and races into the street toward the squirrel. The dog is short. The bus driver does not see it and isn't slowing down enough. We are going to hit the dog. Or worse, we are going to hit the dog *and* the woman about to rush into the street after him. The bus will stop short and all the kids will fly forward, smacking their faces on the seat backs in front of them. This won't end well.

Bailey gasps as she sees the dog leap over the curb. She grabs onto the top of the seat in front of us and tries to stand.

She won't have time to alert the driver, and she knows it.

With a wave of both hands, I send the dog and the woman flying back onto the sidewalk and the squirrel back up its tree. The bus keeps moving forward, all but two of its passengers unaware of what almost happened.

The dog and the woman keep right on walking.

Bailey sits back down, her hand still gripping tight to the seat in front of us. "Okay," she says, breathing quickly, "that was insane."

I am surprisingly calm about the whole thing. It all felt so natural and instinctive. I saw the scene like a movie unfolding behind my eyes, and then I knew what to do.

The bus pulls up to the next stop and Amanda gets on. Her eyes are red-rimmed and puffy. Bailey opens her mouth to call her name, but I put my hand on her arm to stop her. I know when someone doesn't want to talk. "It's okay," I tell her. "Let her go sit with her friends."

As Amanda passes our row, she gives us a strained smile and heads toward the back, where the other eighth graders sit. I wish I knew what she was upset about and if there was any way I could make it better. I watch as she sits down next to Connor. He greets her with a cheerful grunt, then buries his face in the book he's reading.

Bailey is trying to talk to me, but something is happening and it's hard to hear her. The words filling my ears start off softly, not more than a low murmur. Then the murmur turns almost immediately into a roar. It sounds like someone turned on thirty different radio stations at once. It takes a few more seconds until I realize I'm hearing the thoughts of everyone on the bus!

I put my hands over my ears and scrunch down in my seat. Bailey starts shaking my shoulder, but I close my eyes and slide lower. The noise only stops when the bus empties.

I slowly open my eyes and pull my hands away. Bailey is standing over me.

"This has been a REALLY WEIRD BUS RIDE!" she shouts. "What's going on now?"

"Time to get off, girls," the bus driver calls back to us. Bailey grabs both our bags and pushes me down the aisle ahead of her.

"I didn't mean to scare you," I tell Bailey as we make our way into the school. With kids all around us, the noise in my head is deafening. "I can hear everyone's thoughts now. That hasn't happened since the first few days after I woke up from the coma thing."

"You're kind of shouting," Bailey says, glancing around us anxiously.

"Sorry," I reply in a lower voice.

She points to a boy pulling a book from his locker. "What's *that* kid thinking?"

I try to focus on one voice, like tuning in one song on the radio still blaring in my head. My brain hurts from the effort but eventually I can quiet all the other sounds. "He's hoping his mom didn't see him feed his scrambled eggs to the cat."

She points to a girl at the water fountain. "And her?"

"Worried about a spelling test," I reply.

We're in front of Bailey's locker now. "What about me? What number am I thinking of?"

I try to zoom in on her, but I can't. I widen the range and feel around for Connor and the other Team Grace members. I can sense them in different parts of the building but that's all. "I can't read your mind," I tell her, confused. "Or anyone on Team Grace. I can always see a glow around you, but it's like it's more solid now, like a bubble. Oh! Wait! It *is* a bubble! I put it there when I was doing the forgetting spell. It was supposed to protect you."

"Guess it's working!" she says, grinning. "Even if it's only protecting us from you!" She twists open her combination lock. "I wouldn't mind if you could tell my future, though, like you did with the dog running into the street."

"I think that's a different thing," I tell her, forcing myself to focus on just her and not all the background noise. "Stopping the accident felt more natural, like it's what the vortex gave me the power for in the first place. All this . . ." I wave my arms wildly at all the people around us. "All this is overwhelming. I feel like my head is going to split open and everyone's secrets are going to spill out of my ears and onto the floor."

"We'll have to figure out a way to stop it, then," she says, grabbing her books.

"I don't think it's going to be that easy." I struggle to find the words to explain what I've never been good at explaining. "When I first got my powers on my birthday, instead of hearing thoughts, I saw the way everyone and everything was connected to one another. It was beautiful and scary and amazing. But Angelina had to put me in a coma to make it stop before I lost my mind."

I can practically see the gears turning in Bailey's brain as she tries to figure this out. "Okay," she finally says.

"Did you do anything to make it start, whether on purpose or not?"

I think for a second and am about to shake my head when I remember something. "Right before it started, I thought about how I wished I knew why Amanda was so upset."

"Maybe it's that easy!" she says. "You just wish for something and it happens."

I shake my head. "Trust me, I've wished for a lot of things these last few months and mostly what I get is pizza." We're heading toward my locker now, and the halls are starting to thin out. It's getting a little easier to think. Might as well give wishing a try. "Okay," I whisper out loud, "I wish I couldn't hear anyone's thoughts anymore."

I hold my breath for a second, hoping. But no. I can still tell that Suzy from my English class left her book report on the floor of her bedroom and her dog peed on it.

"Did it work?" Bailey asks, leaning forward eagerly.

"No, it did not. And now I have the smell of dog pee in my nose."

"I won't even ask," she says, making a face.

"It's my own fault," I tell her as I struggle to focus on my locker combination. "I wanted my powers to come back stronger, and now that they seem to be, it's more than I want. What if this never goes away? What if Angelina experienced the world this way and just never bothered to mention it to me?"

Bailey reaches over and undoes my lock for me since I seem incapable. "I don't think so," Bailey says. "She would have gone crazy. Even crazier than she is already, I mean. But maybe you can train yourself to only see what you want or need to see."

Angelina said something really similar about training, but I haven't done the gratitude offering that she suggested, or tried to find any ways to either increase or control my powers. "You up for a trip to the library after school?" I ask.

The warning bell rings. "Can't," she says, hurrying toward her homeroom. "Mom's picking me up early for a dentist appointment. Sorry!"

"That's okay, Rory's going to come with me," I blurt out, surprising both of us.

She tilts her head at me. "She is?"

I nod. "I see us walking in together."

"Oh," she says. A flicker of jealousy crosses her face, but she quickly turns it into a smile. "Okay, gotta go! Don't tell anyone their future today."

"Scout's honor," I say, holding up two fingers.

"You aren't a scout," she says, running off in the opposite direction. "And no, being a Sunshine Kid when you were six doesn't count." She gives a final wave and turns the corner.

I feel a little better. It helps that the hallways are almost empty now, so I get a break from the noise and images filling my head. I take a deep breath and walk toward my classroom. *You can do this*, I tell myself. *You can get through this one day*.

Except, I totally can't.

Chapter Eight

GRACE

I can't focus on anything my teacher is trying to teach, and I feel like I'm eavesdropping on everyone and invading their privacy. It helps if I keep my eyes closed, so at least that way I'm not focusing on any one person, but I can't do that in class without getting sent to the principal's office, and I've been there enough for this lifetime.

If I can't find a way to control this, I'm going to wind up hiding under my blanket for the rest of my life with only Green Bunny for company. He has his good qualities, but he isn't a great conversationalist.

By the middle of math, I have reached my breaking point. I raise my hand and ask to go to the nurse. The teacher writes me a pass and tells me to take my books with me.

I walk slowly down to the nurse's office, grateful for the silence of the hall again. The nurse has a bed in a private room behind her office, and I've seen kids resting there while they wait for their parents to pick them up. But I don't want my parents to pick me up. I can't worry them all over again.

While I'm dragging my feet, not sure what to do, a girl steps out of an open classroom door. It's Rory!

"Hey!" she says. "Bathroom run. You?"

"Nurse."

She pulls me away from the classroom so no one can hear us. "Is everything all right? Are you sick?"

I tell her what's going on as quickly as I can, including all the stuff on the bus and the voices and the library and my plan to hide out in the nurse's office.

Rory lets it all sink in, then says, "I used to think Angelina was able to pull these strings that would lead one person to another person or take an event in a certain direction. And I still think that's true, but more than that, she was able to look at all the possibilities of any situation, and single out which one of those would be the best option at the time. Then, somehow, she was able to pull that one thread and make things happen."

I think back to what Rory and Amanda and Tara had told me of their experiences with Angelina, which were all really different. And I think about the things I saw on my birthday, the way it felt like the town was almost a solid blanket made up of people's lives all woven together. Rory could be right.

"Do you think I can do that, too?" I ask her.

"I don't see why not," she says. "Why don't you practice now? You want to quiet the voices in your head. In order to do that, you're pretty sure you need something that's at the library. But in order to make it till after school without losing your mind, you need to be somewhere quiet. Sounds like what you need to do is keep the nurse from calling your parents."

I nod, following along. "Yes, but how?"

"From what I've seen you do so far, and what you said about the bus this morning, you do your best work without thinking too much about how you're doing it."

I nod. She's right. "Okay, let's do it."

Rory walks with me toward the nurse's office. "I'm going to be downtown after school, too," she says. "If you want some company at the library, I'd be happy to go with you."

I smile. Not that I doubted my vision of the two of us walking into the library together, but it's nice to get confirmation. "That would be great. What do you need to do down there?"

She grunts. "Phone store."

I laugh. "What happened to it this time?"

"The screen cracked."

"It fell?"

"Not exactly. I kind of threw it across the room and it hit the wall. Not my finest moment." I notice for the first time how tired she looks, with light purple circles under both eyes.

"Is everything all right?" I ask, feeling guilty that I have only been focusing on my own problems when other people are going through hard things, too.

She sighs. "Just Jake stuff. It's silly."

"It's not silly," I reply. "It's your life. What happened?"

"Well, remember how Jake surprised me with a visit, and we went hiking with my family? Somebody must have recognized him, or been following us or something, and took a picture of him carrying me. *Teen Scene Today* printed it with this obnoxious interview with Madison who said Jake only likes me because he feels sorry for me."

"Ugh, I'm sorry. She's always been jealous, that's all."

We're outside the nurse's office now. "Everyone keeps telling me that," she says, "and I know it's true on one hand, but on the other, maybe she's right. At least a little bit."

"She's not," I say firmly.

"I'm not sure if I'm more upset about that part, or the idea of someone lurking behind a tree taking pictures, ya know? What kind of life is that for him? Having to sneak around, wear disguises, hire look-alikes, or just not go out at all to avoid being followed. It's awful." She lowers her voice. "He doesn't really like being this big teen god. He wants to be a director one day, but he's afraid no one will take him seriously. Plus, if he can't get out and actually experience the world, he's afraid he'll never grow. You know, as a person."

"I totally know how he feels," I say, then wish I could take it back. How am I supposed to know how it feels to be a world-famous teen idol? But I did have a taste of what it feels like when people are always staring at you. I hurriedly add, "I mean, on a much smaller scale, of course. At least he has you, though. He gets to be a normal person with you. He's never had that before. He loves being with you and your family because you like him for who he is on the inside. You always have. He doesn't even know you had a crush on him before you met. You make him feel special in a way no one else has."

She stares at me. "How . . . how do you know all that?"

I pause. How *do* I know it? "I guess this hearing-people's-thoughts-thing works long-distance, too."

Her eyes get all glassy. She reaches out and tugs on my sleeve. "Thanks, Grace."

"This is your shirt," I blurt out.

She laughs. "I recognize it. I wore that shirt the day I tried out to be an extra in the movie. It's a good-luck shirt."

The nurse's door swings open and a boy walks out with a row of Band-Aids on his arm. "Old war wound," he says, holding it up proudly as he passes us.

"Good try!" Rory calls out. "I've used that one before."

"No idea what that means," I say, "but I guess this is where we part ways."

"Do you want me to come in with you?"

I shake my head. "I'll be okay. You should probably get to the bathroom."

"I thought you couldn't read my mind?" she asks.

I smile. "I can't. But you're crossing your legs."

She laughs. "Oh! Yeah, I better go. See you outside the phone store at four?"

"Yup."

She hurries down the hall toward the bathroom. It would be nice if maybe the nurse wasn't in her office, and I could just sneak in and hide in the back room until someone else needed it. But no, she's at her desk filling out paperwork. She doesn't look up when I walk in. She is thinking about a date she has tonight with the new gym teacher and wondering what to wear.

"Um, excuse me?" I say.

She still doesn't look up.

I clear my throat. Loudly.

Nothing.

This is getting weird.

"Um, can I just lay down for a bit in the back?" I ask.

In response, the nurse sticks her pinky in her ear and roots around in there. Yikes, that's kind of gross. I hope she washes that hand before tending to any more war wounds!

It's slowly sinking in that she doesn't see me. I look down at my hands. Yup, still here. I do a jumping jack. Yup, still makes a *thump* when I land, but the nurse doesn't even flinch at the sound. She just keeps thinking about whether her red pumps would send the wrong message and digging around in that ear. Must be a lot of wax in there!

I decide not to push my luck and dart around her desk into the back room. I gently close the door behind me. Ah, it's as quiet as I'd hoped. The only thoughts in my head are my own.

Unfortunately, my victory is short-lived. After only an hour, the nurse leads a sixth-grade boy into the room with a tissue held up to his bloody nose. "Sit on the bed and tilt your head forward," she instructs him. My heart starts racing. He's going to see me!

But he doesn't! He sits down on the bed, only inches away from my face! I don't dare breathe.

"But my mom always has me tilt my head *back* when I get a nose bleed," he argues.

"Your mom is wrong," she snaps. Then she says, "Sorry. I've got a lot on my mind."

"No, you don't," I mutter, sliding down to the end of the bed.

The boy just grunts and tilts his head forward as told. He's hungry and annoyed that he's missing lunch. His being hungry is making *me* hungry. My stomach growls. I've got to get out of here. I slowly climb off the end of the bed and tiptoe around them until the coast is clear. Then I run through the office, nearly toppling a huge bin of Band-Aids.

I don't have to wonder if my seeming invisibility will stick with me out in the hall because the second I run out into it, a kid shouts, "Hey, watch where you're going!" as I barrel right into him. His brown bag lunch goes flying.

"Sorry, sorry!" I yelp, backing out of the way. Then the voices hit me again, and I want to cower in the corner with my hands over my ears. I don't think that will go unnoticed, though, and I'm determined not to cause any more unwanted attention.

Since it's time for lunch, everyone I pass has food on their minds. What they're going to eat, what they're currently eating, what they wish they could eat instead of what's in their bag. It's making me hungrier than I ever remember being. The idea of entering the cafeteria is horrifying, but the hunger, oh, the hunger! So I grab my lunch from my locker and join the throngs streaming in.

I eat my lunch, all the leftovers the kids at my table don't want, and then buy silver-dollar pancakes, a half pint of chocolate milk, and two hot pretzels. I'm late getting back to class, but it's worth it.

I make it through the afternoon, but just barely. As often as I can risk it, I get a bathroom pass and hide out in a stall. By the time I'm back on the bus, I'm completely, utterly exhausted. Since Bailey's mom picked her up, I use our two-seater to curl up and cover my head with the extra sweatshirt I keep in my backpack. Connor has to wake me up when we get to our bus stop.

Chapter Nine

GRACE

I stumble groggily down the bus steps while Connor leaps from the top step and is already on our lawn by the time the bus driver scolds him for jumping. This happens every day.

"Isn't life grand?" he asks, tossing me my backpack, which apparently I'd left on my seat. "Sun is shining, parents are still normal — or as normal as parents can be — and I'm working on a top secret invention that's going to change the way the world sees 3-D movies!"

"Huh?" is pretty much all I can think of to say. Now that I'm home, the quiet in my head is blissful. I think I'm still half-asleep.

Mom meets us at the door with a smile. "Greetings, offspring. How was school today?"

I want to tell her everything, and I can't! That's been the one downside to the whole forgetting thing. Instead, I fall into her arms and hang on. She hugs me back, and I don't let go.

"Now that's the best greeting I've had in months!" she says. "Everything okay, sweetie?"

I nod, relieved that the protective bubble is keeping her mind blank to me. "Just happy to see you!"

She gives me a last squeeze and pulls away. Connor has already disappeared. "Snack? Homework?"

"Actually, I was hoping you could drop me at the phone store? I'm supposed to meet Rory there. She's going to help me work on a project at the library afterward."

"Rory? Oh, that's David Goldberg's friend, right? She was in the play with you."

I swallow past the lump that is forming in my throat. Another hazard of the forgetting spell — Mom no longer remembers how important Team Grace is in my life. Or even that there *is* a Team Grace, even though she was the one who named the group. "Yes," I choke out. "She's great."

"Okay. Grab a snack, and I'll meet you outside."

I probably won't be hungry for a week after the lunch I had, but I don't want to make her suspicious, so I grab a bag of mini-muffins and a juice pouch and wait out in the driveway.

Connor is tinkering away in the garage, the door up to let in the air. I peek in while sipping the juice. "Are those my old costumes?" I ask.

"No," he says, grabbing the muffins from my hand.

I point to the side of the plastic crate next to his work bench. "Then why does it say GRACE'S COSTUMES in big black letters?"

"Oh, those!" he jokes. "Yes, they're your costumes."

I sift through the pieces of old lace scarves and half-broken masks. Bailey and I have pulled apart most of this stuff to make new stuff over the years, so it's not usable for much.

"What do you need these things for?" I ask, slipping on a pair of oversized, pink plastic sunglasses. I strike a pose like a movie star. "No autographs, please."

"Those would be perfect!" he says, grabbing them off my face and taking a few hairs in the process.

"Ouch!" I rub my temple. "You could have just asked."

"Sorry." He holds the glasses up next to a sketch he's made, then he puts them down and starts taking notes. I back away to let him work.

.   .   .   .

Mom drops me off in front of the phone store where Rory is waiting. I introduce them.

"Of course!" Mom says. "Now I remember you from the bar mitzvah party."

"Yes," Rory says after a second's hesitation. "It's nice to see you again."

They chat for a minute about how wonderful a job David did, and Mom says how proud of him she was, and how he's been such a wonderful friend to Connor all these years, and Rory talks about how hard he practiced.

Mom finally says good-bye, and we watch the car pull away without talking. "That was a powerful spell you cast," Rory finally says. "I doubt Angelina herself could have done it any better. She really thinks you guys were at the whole bar mitzvah."

I nod and swallow the lump in my throat.

We walk into the phone store, and everyone starts clapping and cheering and calling Rory's name. I feel like *she* should be wearing those huge, pink, movie star sunglasses! Rory waves them off, laughing. I've heard it's like this when she comes here but have never seen it with my own eyes.

She hands them her cracked phone, and I stand off to the side, listening to their thoughts. Mostly they are trying to figure out which one of them just won the twenty-dollar bet they'd placed on how many days it would be until Rory came in again.

In a few minutes, she's all set. They'd transferred all her data to a new phone and wiped the old one clean. "Wow, that was fast," I say as we head down the street to the library.

"We've got it down," Rory says.

"Do you know they place bets on you?"

She laughs. "Yup. I think it's funny. Sometimes I go in there even when I don't have to, just to mess with them."

I nod in approval. "Nice."

We stop outside the library. "Hey, how did it go at the nurse's?" she asks.

"Apparently I was invisible. She couldn't hear or see me, so I got about an hour before someone else needed the room."

"Nice!" she says, holding up her hand for a high five. "So, what exactly are we looking for in here?"

"I really don't know," I admit. "Angelina was a little vague on that part."

"Why doesn't that surprise me?" she says. "What exactly did she tell you?"

I glance around to make sure no one can hear us. "All she said when I asked how to increase and focus my powers was that I should look in the library."

To Rory's credit, she doesn't ask me when Angelina told me this. That's the kind of person she is. All she says is,

"Well, all right, then. Maybe it's a 'know it when we see it' kind of thing."

We slowly climb the few steps to the library door. "We should check the *V* section first," she suggests. "For *vortex*."

"Good idea," I reply. "Bailey thinks we should look for a secret room hidden in the basement with lanterns lining the halls."

Rory laughs. "That might only be in the movies. Let's look for something a little less obvious."

She swings open the door and we step inside. I point ahead of us. "Something like THAT?"

Not more than five feet in front of us is a big sign that says:

Angelina's Tea Party
Willow Falls Library Storage Room B
4:30 today
Hosted by Rory Swenson and Grace A. Kelly
BYOT (Bring your own tea)
Latecomers will not be admitted.

Clearly Angelina knew exactly when I'd be here and who'd be with me, even if I didn't know it myself. Rory peels the sign off the wall and rolls it up. "Gotta hand it to her. Just when you think she's going to zig, she zags."

"We don't have any tea," I point out as we go in search of Storage Room B. It's not hard to find, seeing as every three feet there's a sign that reads TEA PARTY THIS WAY with an arrow. I tear those down as we go.

"I think the tea is optional," Rory says. She stops in front of a solid wooden door with two masks painted in fading colors — one happy face, one sad. I've seen that symbol before — it was on the playbill for the show Tara produced over the summer.

Rory reaches out to touch the drawing. "I think this used to be the break room where the actors would wait, back when this building was the old playhouse." She pulls out her new phone and checks the time. "Four twenty-nine. Right on time."

I take a deep breath and push open the door. I half expect to see Angelina in there, calmly sipping a cup of tea in a rocking chair, maybe with a ball of yarn on her lap, ready to knit. Isn't that what people do at tea parties?

But the room is completely empty. The only light comes from one flickering lightbulb hanging on a chain from the ceiling. For a storage room, it's not storing anything but dust. Crumbling brick walls surround a cracked gray cement floor. It smells damp. Hopefully it was nicer when the actors used it. Rory and I exchange a glance, then step inside. The door closes behind us and the room bursts into life.

We instinctively huddle close to each other as row after row of bookshelves appear on the now-spotless white walls. The air is filled with the scent of flowers, although I don't see any. Small tables rise up out of the now-gleaming wooden floor, and one by one strange objects appear on their surfaces: a glass ball, a drum, a notebook, a deck of cards, a bowl of what looks like ashes, two metal rods with handles at the ends, six bowls of colored rice, a box of tinfoil, a large purple crystal, a plastic bald head! Rory and I turn in circles, trying to absorb it all.

Only one tabletop remains empty. A second later, a tray appears with two teacups and a plate of chocolate chip cookies. Standing up on the tray is a picture of ancient ruins surrounded by mountains. We head over to the table, and I pick up the photo. It's a postcard. Why am I not surprised?

Chapter Ten

GRACE

Greetings from . . . Machu Picchu!

I flip the card over.

Hello, girls! I'm sorry to miss my own party, but please, help yourselves to tea and cookies. Go on, I'll wait.

The rest of the card is blank. Rory sighs. "Guess we're having tea."

"And cookies!" I add, already biting into one. "It's still warm!"

Rory sips from one of the cups and makes a face. "Needs sugar."

As soon as I take my own sip, words fly across the empty space on the card.

You asked how to increase your energy and control your powers. One of the methods in this room will call to you. I cannot predict which. Listen to it, and it will lead you where you want to go.

"That's all there is," I tell Rory. I'm about to place the card back on the table when more words begin to appear.

Rory Swenson, I'm proud of you. Stay away from those drainpipes.

Rory blushes and chuckles at the same time.
More words appear.

Give Amanda a SpongeBob SquarePants cupcake from the bakery case at the Willow Falls Diner. Tell her you love her. She's having a hard time.

"We will," Rory promises.
I look up from the postcard. "Do you think Angelina can hear us?"
"Who knows?" She bites into her second cookie.
"More is coming," I say, holding it up.

Grace, send Tara into the store. There's something in there she needs. Now get to work. You're running out of time.

The postcard is full. I slide it into my back pocket to add to my collection. "By 'running out of time' does she mean right now? Like, in this room? Or in a larger, more sinister sense?"

"Hard to say," Rory replies.

I haven't forgotten about that feeling I had a few weeks ago, that something big was coming. I don't want to freak Rory out, though, so I change the subject. "And how am I supposed to let Tara in the store when the key doesn't work?"

"Maybe it will now."

"Do you really think so?" I ask. I'd pretty much given up.

"Let's focus on this room first," Rory says. "Where do we start?"

I close my eyes. The table with the plastic head begins to pulse with a white glow. I open my eyes and point to it. "That one."

We position ourselves on either side of the table. Rory waits for me to make the first move.

I lift the head up off the table and take a closer look. Lines and words crisscross the top. "I'm supposed to read the bumps on your head," I say in surprise.

Rory's hands fly to her head. "I have bumps on my head?"

I lean over and feel around her skull. "Hmm . . . your favorite color is purple. . . . You like tomato soup but not tomatoes. . . . You look cute in an eye patch. . . . You —"

"All right, all right," she says, pushing my hands away. "Very funny. We need to take this seriously. Plus, I have no problem with tomatoes."

"How about this one?" I ask, moving over to the tarot cards. I pick up the deck and admire the pastel drawings of various scenes: a boat, a woman with a wand, a sunset. As I watch, the sun in the picture dips lower in the sky, throwing more pink into the scene. I almost drop the card in surprise but manage to hold on.

"Do you see the sun moving?" I ask Rory, holding it out.

She shakes her head.

I hurriedly replace it in the deck. That's just weird.

"What are you supposed to do with these?" Rory asks, holding up the bowl with what looks like burned paper in it.

I dip my fingers into the bowl and close my eyes. "I think I'm supposed to scatter them and then read them."

"Read them?"

"The way they fall is supposed to tell us something." I toss the ashes into the air while saying, "Oh, mysterious ashes, please guide us toward what we seek." The ashes flutter around us. A few land on the table, but most fall to the floor.

"Um, you're sure that's right?" Rory asks, sliding a few out of her hair. "Kinda just looks like a mess."

I examine the ones at my feet. They almost look like they're forming a line, or an arrow. I circle around the pile. Yes, definitely an arrow. Only it's pointing directly between two of the tables, one with the metal rods on it and the other with the box of tinfoil.

"It's one of those two," I tell Rory. "Or maybe it's both."

"Let's try the tinfoil first," she suggests.

I pick up the box and see directions printed on it. "It says we're supposed to make tinfoil hats to help us tune into the energy around us better. Cool!"

Rory looks doubtful about its coolness, but says, "Luckily, I'm an expert tinfoil hat maker. Sawyer has a whole collection. Pirate hat? Top hat? Chef's hat? I can do 'em all."

"How about a pointy hat?"

"Like a witch?"

"Sort of . . ." I examine the picture more carefully. "More like a traffic cone."

"Those orange ones?"

"Yup."

"I'll do my best," she says, getting to work.

I leave her to the hats and move onto the rods. They look like skinny, oversized candy canes, except the handle at the top is straight so it looks like an uppercase *L*. When I pick one up by the handle, the rod swings gently side to side, while the handle stays firmly in my hand.

Dowsing rods. The name comes to me from some ancient place. *A tool to find hidden water, treasure, or energy sources.*

"Energy sources!" I say out loud.

"Hmm?" Rory asks, busy with her sheets of foil.

I hold up the rods. "I'm supposed to find the vortex," I announce. "With these!"

The moment I wave the rods in the air, the room goes back to the way it was before. "Ouch," Rory says, bonking her head on the swinging lightbulb that has reappeared directly above her head. "Was that always so low?"

I laugh. "You must be getting taller."

"Doubtful," she mutters.

I turn in a circle. "Everything's gone. And all those books! We didn't even get a chance to look at them."

"Not everything. I've still got these." She holds up her hands to reveal two perfect cone-shaped tinfoil hats.

"How did you do that so fast?"

"It wasn't that fast," she replies. "You were swinging those rods for a while."

I was? It didn't feel like more than a few seconds.

She plops one of the hats on my head and gamely puts on the other. As soon as the hat settles on my head, I know that something's different. All the while we've been in the room, I'd been hearing the muffled thoughts of the other people in the library. It had been so low, I'd been able to ignore it. But now it was completely gone.

I start jumping up and down. "No more voices!" I shout.

"Except yours!" Rory says. "Library, ya know!"

Oops!

"But totes awesomesauce for you!" she says. "Is that how you say it?"

I laugh. "Yup." Grinning like I've just won the lottery, I stick the dowsing rods in my back pocket the way Amanda carries her drumsticks. We make our way out of the library, turning many heads as we go. I check the time on my phone. It's almost six. "I better text my mom. She's supposed to pick me up in five minutes."

"Tell her to meet you at the diner," Rory suggests. "I'll go with you so I can get Amanda's cupcake."

I send Mom the message, and we head down the street. Every single person stares at us. It doesn't take a mind reader to know they're wondering why we're wearing pointy tinfoil hats. It feels like it did before the forgetting spell when everyone was staring at me all the time, but at least now I'm not alone.

"Just hold your head high," Rory whispers. "Sometimes I'd rather duck and hide, like when an article comes out about Jake. But you have to act like it doesn't bother you. I'm hoping if I pretend long enough, one day it won't."

I nod and do my best to tell myself I *don't* have a silver cone on my head. Once it's off, no one will point at me again, but Rory won't be so lucky. You can't live in a small town and escape unnoticed when you're friends with a movie star.

"Do you have any idea where the vortex actually is?" she asks.

I shake my head. The hat almost falls off, and I have to straighten it. "Angelina never told me. In fact, I don't really know anything about the vortex at all."

"Bucky told us a little about it," she says, "that night when Amanda and Leo went back to Angelina's eighteenth birthday party. I don't remember the details, though. He may have said the vortex is on the outskirts of town somewhere? We should get Amanda and Leo together, and Tara, too. Maybe one of them remembers something."

"Sounds good," I reply, and we keep walking. We reach the diner, and I can see through the glass windows that a whole bunch of girls from Rory's grade are sitting in the booths. Rory sees them, too, and slows down before they see us. Just then, both our phones ding with a text.

"It's from Tara," Rory says, reaching for hers first. She begins to read it out loud. "'My mother just drove past you guys on Main Street. She said to take off those ridiculous hats this instant, and that somewhere Angelina is getting a good laugh.'"

Rory looks up from the phone. "You think she's right?"

"Tara's mom knows Angelina better than either one of us does," I reply. Still, I hesitate before taking it off. What if the voices come back? Ever so slowly, I lift it off my head. Ah, still quiet. I say a silent thank you to Angelina. The hat may look silly, but it did its job. I fold it down until it fits in my pocket.

Rory crosses her arms. "I'm going to keep mine on just in case Mrs. Brennan is wrong and it will help you somehow. Plus, I've been embarrassed *way* worse than this in my day!"

"That's the spirit! Now, go get that cupcake!"

"I will!" Rory says, chin up, head high. She glances at the booths, takes a deep breath, and steps inside.

That girl is SPECIAL.

TARA

Dear Julie,

I'm typing this to you on my phone while I'm sitting on a stranger's curb around the corner from my house, and then I'll print it out and mail it tomorrow. My dad asked me the other day why you and I don't just email each other instead of finding paper / finding a pen that works / finding envelopes / finding stamps / and dropping it in a mailbox, but it wouldn't feel right. We're *pen pals*, I told him, not email pals! And writing real letters is a lost art, anyway, right?

So right now, me = riding in circles in my neighborhood with my headphones on. I love having my bike back because everything in this new town has been, well, NEW. My clothes, my house, my friends, my boyfriend, my school, my cousin Emily and her family, and even having a semi-normal relationship with my mom is new. I don't mean to sound like I'm complaining, because it's more than I ever dreamed I'd get in a hundred lifetimes, but THAT'S A LOT OF NEW. My dad told me last night how I'm adjusting so well to life here, and I feel like I am, most of the time, but then other times I just want to get on my bike and ride, ride, ride and shut everything out. I don't want my friends here to know that I feel like this sometimes. I'm so grateful that you and I are in touch again.

Hang on, a call from my mom coming in.

Okay, just had to send a text to Grace and Rory, who for some reason are wearing funny hats in public. I've got to admit, life in Willow Falls is never boring. Well, I only have a little while to ride and then I'm going over to my cousin's house. She's going to show me how to fence. She says I'd be good at it because I'm so tall. Honestly, I'm not so sure I'm particularly good at anything. I think I just need to keep riding and stop grizzling! (That's an Australian expression Ray says whenever he hears me complaining!)

w/b/s

Your friend Tara, who is in a weird mood

CONNOR

CONNOR KELLY'S INVENTOR'S JOURNAL
Type of product: 3-D Glasses for Glasses Wearers
Inventor: Connor Kelly
Description of invention-in-progress: So apparently the process of turning a television screen into 3-D is more complicated than I had at first suspected — there's all this stuff about polarization, and tricking the eye into viewing two slightly different images at once, etc., etc., which I guess explains why no one has done it yet, or done it well. I was ready to throw in the towel (that's inventor lingo for quit) when my beta tester (and best friend) David Goldberg and I started talking about it over lunch at school. I hadn't told anyone my idea for the screen yet, but David kept asking if there's anything he could do to make my life better because

he's practicing this whole "pay it forward" thing, so I explained my problem to him, and he said that he doesn't really like to go to 3-D movies because it's uncomfortable to wear the glasses they give you over his real glasses. DING DING DING! That's the sound of a bell going off in my head. I can invent 3-D glasses for glasses wearers!

What problem does it solve: This product would solve the problem of eyeglass wearers having to either take off their glasses to fit on the 3-D frames and deal with the decline in their vision, or suffer the discomfort of wearing both pairs at once.

Who will want or need this product: 3-D moviegoers who wear prescription eyeglasses.

Materials: 3-D glasses with lenses removed, oversized frames I snagged from my sister

Steps: Analyze existing 3-D glasses frames, build my own pair complete with working lenses.

Results: Fingers still crossed at this point!

Final observations: I'll tell ya when it's done!

Notes: David joined me in the garage, and the last few hours have been very productive. Between the two of us, we were able to come up with six pairs of the kind of 3-D glasses you get in the theatre. Unfortunately, none of the lenses are big enough for the oversized frame I want to set them in. I tried to melt them down so I could make larger ones, but all it did was bubble and blacken. So I borrowed a roll of cellophane from the kitchen, which hopefully Mom won't miss tonight when she's putting away leftovers. Then I took out the lenses from Grace's huge sunglasses (which was easy because they are very cheap glasses and the lenses popped right out). I laid the lenses on the cellophane and traced around them. Then I cut the circles out and tried to color one red and one blue, but it was a mess, so I realized I should color them *before* I cut them out. So I repeated my first steps, but this time colored one with red marker, and one with blue marker, *then* cut them out. Then I taped the thin colored pieces of cellophane onto the glasses where the lenses were. This does not look pretty, but I tested it out on a 3-D comic book I have, and it totally worked.

My beta tester said that the oversized frames allowed the stems (the side parts that go behind your ears) of the new glasses to extend farther past his ears than previous pairs, so they didn't touch his own glasses. This is good. But then he complained that the bridge of the glasses still rested on his own glasses in an uncomfortable way. So now I am extending the bridge of the glasses so they rest on the nose *in front of* regular glasses.

Roger said I could come over tonight to show him my progress. Have to go inside now for a snack. Inventing makes a guy hungry!

DAVID

To: Linda@OnlineFamilyTherapy.com
From: DavidGoldberg@WillowFallsSchool.edu
Subject: Walk on a Fall Evening

Hey there, Linda, old buddy, old pal. Just had to write to tell you about something cool that happened today. After an early dinner, I was taking a walk with my dad. (Which, by the way, is a sentence that I never thought I'd ever get to write — but that's not the cool thing I wanted to tell you.) So anyway, we were turning the corner of our street when a girl on a bike zoomed by. She was going so fast she was almost a blur. I didn't pay much attention because I was focused on enjoying the walking-with-Dad part, but then he nudged me and said, "Wasn't that your girlfriend?" And he didn't say it in a teasing kind of "nudge-nudge you have a girlfriend" way, which is one of the many cool things about him.

I shielded my eyes with my hand and peered down the street, but the girl was already gone.

"I'm pretty sure it was Tara," he said.

"Wouldn't she have stopped if she saw us, though?" I asked as a cold chill rose up my spine. (By the way, Linda, I don't usually say things like *a cold chill rose up my spine*, but that's how it felt, and if you can't be honest with your therapist, then what's the point of therapy?) Anyway, where was I? Oh, right, so now I'm all worried that maybe Tara's mad at me for something, and I try to think of what I could have done. Had I been spending too much time with Connor? Or my dad? Had I not helped her settle into town enough? Had I messed this up??

"Breathe," Dad said, shaking me. "I'm sure she just didn't see us. She seemed pretty focused."

Before I can explain my fears, the girl comes whizzing down the street toward us again. This time she puts on the breaks and slows down enough for us both to recognize each other.

"Hey," she says, yanking off her helmet and shaking out her hair. (Did I ever tell you she has really pretty hair? I probably didn't. She does, though.)

Dad gave us both pats on our arms and said, "I've gotta run. Forgot to feed the dog."

"We don't have a dog," I reminded him.

He winked and strode away toward the house. I turned back to Tara, who was pulling out her earbuds. I almost said one of a few corny lines from movies that popped into my head, like "What's a nice girl like you doing in a place like this?" or "Funny meeting you here" or "Looks like it's just you and me, kid." But she probably didn't have to sit through as many movies with her mom as I did over the years, and I would've sounded weird. So instead, I rambled something dorky about it being a nice night for a ride.

Then she said, "I'm sorry, but I'm in kind of a weird mood. Probably shouldn't be around people."

"Is it anything to do with me?" I asked, holding my breath a little.

She shook her head. "Just overwhelmed, I think. I'm trying to ride it out."

"You're sure?" I asked, because I've learned that sometimes girls might not tell you things the first time you ask. I know that sounds bad, but it's kind of true.

"Positive," she said.

There might have been the slightest of hesitations, but I decided to take her at her word. How could she not be overwhelmed in her situation? I needed to step up the boyfriend thing by both being there for her and also giving her space. "Is it working?" I asked. "The biking, I mean?"

"Maybe a little," she said.

"I know something that will help," I told her. So she walked her bike between us, and I led her right to her cousin's backyard and into the pool hole where I used to practice for my bar mitzvah. We didn't take the bike down, obviously. "Everyone should have a place to be alone," I told her as we looked up at the sky turning pink above us. "This place always calmed me down. Now it's yours. You know, until your aunt and uncle get around to putting water into it!"

She looked unsure, but I settled her into a cozy corner and said, "Trust me, a little while down here in the earth listening to music and you'll feel good as new."

She stuck her earbuds back in her ears. "I'm listening to you," she said, fiddling with the buttons on her phone.

So I said, "Good. Trust me, the pool hole always works."

She shook her head. "No, I mean I'm listening to *you*." She points to her ears. "In my head. The recording you made me for my birthday. You're singing to me."

Well, Linda, I gotta tell you. My face got all hot, and my legs felt a little shaky when she said that. Of all the songs in the world, she picked mine to make her feel better. So what happened next, you ask? Well, Linda. That's rated

PG-13, if you know what I mean. Wink-wink. Then Tara only had a few minutes before she had to be inside, so I left her to be on her own, which was really the point in the first place.

Thanks for listening to my story, Linda. One nice thing about never actually sending you these emails is that I don't get charged $$. So it's a win-win!

Sincerely yours,

David Goldberg

Chapter Eleven

GRACE

I call Tara right after dinner. She picks up on the first ring.

"I hope someone took a picture of you guys with those hats on," she says instead of hello.

I laugh. "Nope, sorry. You'll have to use your imagination."

"Bummer. I was hoping to get you back for that picture you took of us in those Sunshine Kid uniforms."

I remember the day I first met Tara and Amanda and Rory when they rang our bell selling cookies. Could that have been only a few months ago? Crazy! "Thanks for the reminder to print that out! Someday you'll have to tell me the story behind it. But for now, guess what?"

She sighs. "In this town it could be anything. I give up. Wait, before you tell me, let me put down the sword Emily just gave me. We're practicing for my first fencing class."

I hear some shuffling and a muffled "Ouch," and "Careful!" and "Sorry!" and then she's back. "Okay, lay it on me."

"Are you free to do something tomorrow morning?" I ask.

"Amanda's mom is coming over to help my mom decorate," she says. "They keep asking me if I like this paint color or that carpet fabric, and I keep saying yes, and then they change it anyway. So, yes, I'd love an excuse not to be home."

"Good! Then we have a date at Angelina's Sweet Repeats and Collectibles at ten o'clock."

"We do?"

"Yup. Angelina said there's something you need in there."

Silence. "You spoke to Angelina?"

"Yes! Well, sort of. Not exactly. Okay, it was through a postcard."

More silence.

"You okay?" I ask.

She finally says, "Did I do something wrong, do you know?"

"I'm sure you didn't," I try to assure her. "But it must be really important for her to have mentioned it, right?"

"I'm not going to sleep tonight," she says, and I can tell from her breathing that she's pacing the room. "What if we went there now?"

I look at the clock in my room. It's seven already, not usually the time I'd be going out with my friends. It's a Friday night, though, so it's not like I have to get up early for school tomorrow. "I guess we could go tonight. But my mom will probably say anything I could do now I could do tomorrow instead."

"How about this," she says. "I'm already at my aunt and uncle's hanging out with Emily, and your brother is upstairs with my uncle in the lab. What if Connor needed you to drop something over here, and then Ray brought us to the store and offered to take you both home?"

I consider her idea. "*Does* Connor need something?"

"I don't know; I'll go ask him. Hang on."

I hear shuffling, then muffled voices. A minute later she comes back and says, "Connor would like a Three Musketeers bar."

"A Three Musketeers bar?" I repeat.

"Yes. He says your mom has a bag in the closet for Halloween. He says it's urgent. Something about how he needs to measure the thickness of the nougat for his invention."

Yeah, I'm not buying that for a second, but I let it go. "And Ray said he'd take us?"

"Actually, he said, 'No worries, mate.'"

"Okay, I'll tell my parents Ray's going to pick me up, so have him swing by in five minutes."

"Will do," she says. "And thanks. I think!"

It's easier than I would have thought to convince my parents to let me go off with Ray. They know and trust him from directing the play, and he's dropped Connor off after work before. Plus his accent would charm anyone.

Fifteen minutes later, I'm unzipping the pouch that I retrieved from my desk drawer and tossing Connor his chocolate bar in the middle of the St. Claires' living room. I've never been in their house before, even though it's right across the street from David's, where I've been tons. The house is very clean and modern. As I suspected, Connor tears open the candy bar wrapper and begins to chew.

"So when do I get to see your invention?" I ask him while Tara searches Emily's room for her shoes. According to her, as neat as the rest of the house is, that's how messy her cousin's room is.

"Roger has it upstairs in his lab," he says.

"You call him Roger?" I ask.

He nods. "We inventors are laid-back dudes. No suits and ties and formal names for us."

"So basically you don't want to show me."

"Righto," he says, and shoves the rest of the candy bar in his mouth. Then he smiles really wide so I can see the layer of chocolate coating his teeth. It will likely be many years until Connor gets a girlfriend.

We have to pass Bailey's house on the way to the store, and Ray agrees to stop so I can invite her to come. After all her trips to the store with me, if we actually get inside and she's not with me, I'd feel terrible.

As Tara and I walk up to the door, I send a message in my head to Bailey's mom so she'll let Bailey come out with us. It must have worked because just as we're about to ring the bell, Bailey runs out in her pj's and flip-flops. "Be home by nine!" her mom calls out after her.

On the way into town, I tell them about today's adventure at the library. They all request a picture of the hats. I groan. "Forget the hats. Focus on the important part."

"So you're supposed to use those metal sticks to somehow find the vortex?" Tara asks. "And then what?"

Ray parks the car on Main Street and we climb out. "I have no idea," I admit. "Angelina said something about a gratitude offering. I don't know what that is, though."

We start down the alley. The sun is setting, and a golden glow bounces off the cobblestones. "Once when I was a wee ankle biter," Ray says, "I visited the outback with my oldies and saw people offering gratitude to their spirit animals. They were sprinkling grass seeds or nuts or rice, then they gave thanks for guidance and protection."

"What's a spirit animal?" Tara asks. I have no idea, either.

"You pick an animal to protect you, or rather it picks you," he explains. "It's supposed to embody your essence or some mumbo jumbo like that. Give you power and strength."

"But I don't have a spirit animal."

"You can pick one," he says. "How about a penguin?"

"Seriously?"

"What do you have against penguins?" he asks. "They're like really big birds in tuxedos. They're always ready for a fancy dance."

"I don't have anything against them, but I don't really have anything *for* them." I think about the ceramic bunny Amanda painted for me that sat by my bed. Maybe that would be good. But we're in front of the store now, so spirit animals or lack of them will have to wait. "Ready, Tara?"

She presses her face to the large glass window. "Can you see anything?" she asks. "I mean, like is anything strange or unusual going on in there?"

I peer through the window. When Tara first showed me the store — the very first day I awoke from the coma — the objects told me their stories, just like the voices of all the people I'd heard at school. All the clothes, sports equipment, faded paintings, toys. I could tell where they'd come from, why they were brought here, and where they were headed. But on every visit since, the items have been annoyingly silent. I shake my head. "Looks the same as the last time we were here."

"That's good, I guess," Tara says. "So what am I supposed to look for?"

"I bet you'll know it when you see it," Bailey says.

"Maybe." She starts to chew her nail, then stops. "Picked that up from Amanda. We hear the name Angelina and start biting our nails!"

"You guys really think we'll get in?" Ray asks, jiggling the doorknob.

"Not *that* way." I bat his hand away. "Hang on." I hand Tara the pouch with the key. She holds it out in front of her like it's going to bite.

I reach up and put my hand on her shoulder. "If we get in there and you want to leave, we'll leave, okay?"

She nods. "Okay. Here goes." She takes out the key and hands the pouch to Bailey, who tries to stick it in her pocket, but her pocket's too small. All of Angelina's postcards are still in there from when I hid them from Mom, so she tucks it in her sock instead.

Tara closes her eyes, breathes, then puts the key in the lock, hesitates for only a second, and turns it.

Click.

Ray and I exchange a look of surprise. I think we were both thinking it probably wouldn't work after all.

Tara pushes open the door, and the four of us stand at the threshold. "You first," I tell her. She shakes her head. "You."

"I'm game," Ray says, and walks right through. I cringe a little, half expecting some force field to zap him, or a net to grab him and string him upside down by his ankles, but it's pretty uneventful. He finds the light switch on the wall and flicks it.

Nothing happens. He flicks it up and down a few times, but the room remains bathed in only the dusky sunset. "Guess Angelina forgot to pay the electric bill," Ray jokes.

"Well, that won't make this any easier," Tara says, stepping in. Bailey and I hurry behind her. Tara begins winding her way through the piles, running her hands along various objects.

"I can't believe I'm in here!" I shout. "I'm inside the store!" I wave my arms around and twirl. Bailey joins me and we do a part of our routine from *Fiddler* where we link arms and switch places like a square dance for two.

"Whoa there, little misses," Ray says, grabbing for a coat rack covered with hats and scarves that almost topples into the aisle. "There's a lot of breakable stuff in here."

"Sorry!" Bailey says, righting a lampshade that had gotten caught on her foot.

I look around the room, trying to make out what I can in the ever-increasing darkness. The stuff looks the same inside as it did from the window, only dustier. I pick up an old Magic 8 Ball from a bin full of dented plastic toys. Years ago, Connor and I found one of these in Mom's old toy chest from when she was a kid. We played with it for a few months before Connor decided to smash it to see what was inside. The blue stain on Mom's favorite rug is still there six years later.

"Will Tara find what she's looking for?" I ask the 8 Ball, then turn it right-side up.

"What does it say?" Bailey asks, peering over my shoulder.

I have to shine my phone light on it to read the response in the little round window. "It says, 'Concentrate and ask again.'"

"Figures," Bailey says.

But I close my eyes, take a deep breath, and picture a glow around whatever Tara is supposed to find. I open my eyes, intending on shaking the 8 Ball to find the answer, but I no longer need to see what it says.

Because in the far corner of the room, underneath a rolled-up carpet and a giant polka-dotted stuffed giraffe, is a box. It looks like an ordinary cardboard box with TO DONATE written across the side. But the light shining out of it fills the room.

Chapter Twelve

GRACE

"There," I call out, pointing. Tara is too far across the room to hear me. I move toward her. "There," I repeat, louder this time. She puts down the globe of the world she'd been admiring and follows my finger.

"I still don't see anything," she says.

Okay, so I guess the light is just for me. I still haven't come close to figuring out the rules of why sometimes everyone can see what I see, and sometimes I'm alone in it all. But now's not the time to dwell on it. I head toward the source of the light and the others follow.

Ray lifts off the carpet, Bailey grabs the giraffe, and Tara slides out the box.

"I've seen this box before!" she says, examining the outside. "See? It's from a store back in my last town. And

167

that's my dad's handwriting on the side. He must have donated this stuff when we moved, and it wound up here somehow."

"Why would Angelina want you to take your own stuff back?" Bailey asks.

"No idea," Tara says. "Let's find out." She lifts the flaps and holds them open. We all peer in. Ray and Bailey shine their phones down on it, but I can see the contents perfectly clearly thanks to the white glow still surrounding the box.

"My dad's old books?" she says. She pulls them out one by one and piles them on the floor beside her. "I saw him gathering these when we went back to the old house a few weeks ago. They're just books from his office that he doesn't need anymore. He has duplicates of most of them."

Bailey picks one up from the top of the pile. It's a well-worn dictionary. I glance at the others. Mostly they seem to be paperback novels and some books on the kind of subjects you'd expect a science fiction writer to have: *Life in the Universe*, *The Spaceflight Handbook*, *Things That Go Bump in the Night*.

Tara lifts the last two books out of the box and tries to separate them. Flakes of dried glue fall to the floor. She twists the books until they finally fly apart. One of the books looks like it has pages slipping out. Tara notices, too, and pulls at the pages. What comes away in her hand is a book made out of glued-together pages. Bailey shines her phone light onto it and Tara starts laughing. "It's a book my dad wrote for me when I was in third grade! We all thought it had been thrown out by mistake years ago. It must have been stuck in here the whole time."

She holds the handmade book closer to the light and reads the brightly colored words on the cover: *The Day Tara the Great Destroyed the Zombie Queen and Then Ate a Grilled Cheese Sandwich.*

We all laugh at the title.

"Dad used to let me illustrate the covers of the books he wrote for me," Tara says, touching the picture of a girl in a multicolored dress stomping on an oozing zombie. The girl is adjusting her crown with one hand, while eating half a grilled cheese sandwich with the other.

Tara lays the book on her lap. "It's awesome to have it back, but is this really what Angelina meant?"

"I guess it must be," I say, glancing at the discarded books. "There's nothing else in the box, right?"

Tara looks back down at the handmade book like she's not quite sure whether to be disappointed or happy that she got off easy. Ray steals away and starts swinging some golf clubs he found.

"Can I see it?" Bailey asks.

Tara hands the book to her, and Bailey starts reading through it.

"Tara," Bailey says slowly, "This is really, really good. Like publishable good. Like kind of brilliant and hilarious."

She smiles. "My dad spins a great tale."

"No," Bailey says. "*You* do."

Tara begins putting the other books back in the box. "Pretty sure my artwork isn't going to be hanging in museums one day."

"But you didn't just draw the cover," Bailey says.

"Yeah, there are a few drawings inside, too," Tara says.

Bailey holds the book out to Tara. "I mean you didn't only illustrate it, you wrote it, too."

Tara furrows her brows. "What do you mean?"

"Look," Bailey says, holding open the book to the first page.

Written and Illustrated by Tara Brennan, age 9.

Tara inhales sharply, then takes the book and starts reading it.

"Do you remember writing it?" I ask.

She shakes her head. "No." Then, "Maybe? I'm not sure. But if I could write like this, why would my parents keep that from me?"

I sit beside her and touch the open pages. The whole story comes flying out at me. "Your mother hid it," I blurt out. "Your dad was going to enter it into a national writing contest for kids. She was so used to trying to keep Angelina from finding you that she couldn't take the chance that you'd win and be in the news."

Tara's jaw drops.

"Your mom always meant to tell you, but she sort of . . . forgot? No one could find the book, and it became easier to think she'd overestimated how good the book was, that it was probably just a typical story a smart nine-year-old would write. You hadn't written anything since, so that made it easier to believe you weren't interested anymore." I let out a deep breath. "That's all I got."

Tara is shaking her head. "I *did* write," she insists. "Only they weren't stories. I wrote letters. Dozens and dozens and dozens of long letters with stories about my childhood, or just life in general. My parents didn't know about them, though."

She turns her attention back to the book and begins reading it to herself, laughing and crying and shaking her head. Bailey signals me to back away and give Tara privacy. She goes off to find Ray, bumping into a rocking chair and knocking over a shelf of plastic action figures. I head toward the counter in the back, where an object sitting beside the cash register has caught my eye.

A silver ribbon encircles the top of a small gauze bag filled with what looks like tiny brown seeds. I lift it up and feel the nice heft of it. Under the bag is a card. *Greetings from . . . Sedona, Arizona!*

That old gal gets around! I turn it over. There are only a few sentences:

The wheels are in motion, and they will only move forward. I can see it all the way from here. Do not forget, life is a dance between making things happen and letting things happen. I do not envy you your choice.

It doesn't make any more sense the second and third time I read it over. I'm about to show it to the others when I feel a jolt, and the air ripples around me in invisible waves. I have to grab onto the edge of the counter to keep from falling over. The sensation lasts only a few seconds, and when it's done the room feels . . . different somehow. What the heck was *that?*

I take deep gulps of air to steady myself and scan the room for my friends. I see Bailey first, coming toward me. Before I can ask if she's all right, she holds up a pink silk dress and asks, "Do you think I can have this?"

When I'm too surprised to answer, she goes on. "I

would take out these dorky shoulder pads of course, and I'd move the lace from the arms to the —"

I finally interrupt her. "Didn't you feel that?"

"Feel what?" she asks, draping the dress over one shoulder.

Ray joins us, the bag of golf clubs under one arm and a box with old theatre playbills under the other. Tara is next, clutching her book in one hand and the huge giraffe in the other. She holds it up. "I think my cousin Emily would like this."

Ray says, "Hey, Grace, how do you feel about giraffes? Majestic creatures, really. Did you know they have four stomachs? You could do a lot worse for a spirit animal."

I look from one to the other. "Hold on. None of you felt like you were caught in a wave of air just then? Like everything shimmered and then settled a little differently?"

They each shake their heads, exchanging glances. "Are you okay?" Bailey asks.

I nod slowly, not wanting to worry them. "Being around all this stuff must have made me dizzy. We should go."

The three of them make their way back to the front, following one another closely so no one trips in the dark. When they pass the coat rack that I almost knocked down earlier, Tara grabs a tall top hat and sticks it on Ray's head.

They all laugh. They definitely don't sense anything is different. I still feel unsettled, though. Wish I knew what it was.

The postcard is still in my hand. I stick it in my pocket and pick up the bag of seeds from the floor where I must have dropped them. I don't know what happened back there, but it makes me even more determined to find the vortex. If wheels are in motion, I'll need to know how to stop them before they crash into whatever they're heading toward.

I'm the last one out. I close the door behind me and check that it's locked. Then I glance inside one last time. The glow around Tara's box has faded, but when combined with the light from the street lamp, I can see inside pretty well. I gasp and drop the bag of seeds again.

Half the items in the store are gone.

AMANDA

Dear Diary,

Something really weird happened a few minutes ago. I'm writing this in the car on the way home from seeing Stephanie's gymnastics meet, so I'm sorry if it's messy. I thought that going would help me take my mind off things, and I loved watching Stephanie compete (Ruby, not so much), and Tracy and Emma called me over to sit with them in the bleachers, which was really nice because I haven't hung out with them in a long time. It felt like old times. But even still, I kept wanting to send Leo a video of Stephanie's awesome back handspring or text him a picture of the bag of candy Emma brought with her. But I didn't feel like I had the right to.

Anyway, so right near the end of the competition, I felt this weird cold breeze, as if a door was open right next to me. But it's not cold out. And there was no door. Then, after it passed, something felt sort of *off*, like kind of different. I don't know how to explain it. I asked the twins if they felt anything, but they didn't. I can't shake it, though. Since our eleventh birthday, whenever anything magical has happened in town, like with Rory or Tara or Grace, Leo and I have been able to sense it. It felt almost like that, but not exactly like it. I guess Grace would have contacted us if anything big had happened.

The pointer finger on my right hand is bleeding because I chewed the nail too far down. Grossness.

Right now we're passing through Main Street, past the diner and the paint-your-own-pottery place. Lots of memories at that place but I push them aside. I feel even more uneasy as Mom's car nears the corner where you'd turn to walk down the alley.

Okay, I had to put down my pen for a second to catch my breath. I'm sure my handwriting is even worse now because when we passed the alley, the car headlights shone down it a little, and I saw that the watch store on the corner was gone. Like, gone gone. Like, no longer there AT ALL.

I have to tell the others.

Or maybe stores close down all the time and it's no big deal? I mean, I never saw anyone ever go into that store, or the barbershop, either. That's probably it, just a store closing and they knocked it down because it was old and not structurally sound or whatever. Or maybe my eyes were playing tricks on me.

We're almost home, and I'm really tired. I'll figure it out in the morning.

RORY

Rory: You will NOT BELIEVE the cool thing that just happened!!!

David: Try me. Takes a lot to surprise me these days.

So Jake just called me.

OMG! Jake Harrison the movie hottie? Total awesomesauce!

Haha very funny. And it's *totes* awesomesauce. But let me finish!

Sorry, couldn't resist. I've missed you!

I know. I've missed you, too.

Our lives sure have changed over the last year. Both of us going out with someone? I mean, I knew it would happen for you, but I figured I'd have my first date sometime around college!

Lol. Tara is really great and I'm really happy for you and I'm really glad you and I are still friends.

That's a lot of "really's," but me, too. And I'm sorry that I was kind of self-absorbed these last few months with my dad and all, and a little hyper, but I'm just really happy. So ya gonna tell me what I'm not going to believe, or what?

Oh yeah, so GET THIS! Jake had to go into the supermarket near his house to get something for his mom. She was stuck on an important phone call, otherwise he would NEVER go into a supermarket alone.

Yeah, supermarkets can be scary places. I was at the Willow Falls Organic Market last week, and a frozen hamburger patty turned back into a cow and attacked me! Right there in Aisle 9!

Sigh. Do you want to hear this or not??

Sorry, yes, more than anything.

While I'm pretty sure that's not true, I'm going to tell you anyway. Okay, so there he is in the supermarket, and since this was a last-minute thing, he didn't have any of his disguises or any bodyguards. So what do you think happened?

Pretty sure I know this answer. He was mobbed by screaming girls while paparazzi swarmed around him taking pictures. Moms followed him through the aisles, piling up their carts with all the same things he bought so they could tell their teenage girls later that night that they're eating the very same meal as Jake Harrison. Am I right?

Wrong on all counts. NOTHING HAPPENED!

What do you mean? Like, no cows came to life?

I mean Nothing Happened! No one even gave him a second glance!!!

Was this market in a parallel universe where no one knew him?

Nope! Just a regular supermarket.

Did he have a baseball cap covering his face?

Nope. People must have finally gotten the message that he's more than just a pretty face!

He said it was like . . .

Magic!

Yes!

No, I mean it WAS magic!

What do you mean?

I mean, there's no way heads aren't going to turn when the star of the biggest movie of the summer comes into a supermarket. Grace must have done it.

OMG, you're right!!!!

The Hamburglar is never wrong.

GTG, thanks!

. . . .

Rory: OMG did you fix it somehow so Jake can go out in public without being recognized?

Grace: Maybe.

You did?! OMG, I'm crying. I can barely see to type. How can I thank you? Why did you do it? *How* did you do it?

I kept thinking about what you said the other day about how hard it was for Jake, and you were so kind to drop everything and come with me to the library when you were dealing with Madison and her mean comments, and I thought if only there was a way to make it so that when Jake didn't want to be recognized, he wouldn't be. It's called a glamour. It's like a mask he puts on so he looks different to other people.

Like when Amanda and Leo went back in time to your birthday parties!

Yes! That's how I knew I could do it, since Angelina had done it to them. He's not really changing or anything. He still looks like himself, except when he doesn't want to.

I'm going to need to tell him. He'll eventually realize it's not a coincidence that he keeps going out and not being bothered by fans.

I know.

THAT will be an interesting conversation!!

I think he's ready for it.

I think you're right. I love you for doing this. I know it's not as big a deal as giving David his dad and grandfather back, but it's going to change his life, and mine!

You're welcome. XOXO

Enough about me! How are YOU doing?

Good. Working some things out. I hope it doesn't take too long to find the vortex once we're all together.

Have you tried on your own?

A few times on my front lawn. I held onto the handles with the rods right in front of me, but the ends didn't move, no matter what direction I turned in. They're supposed to swivel toward what you're looking for. Wherever the vortex is, it must be too far from my house for the rods to pick it up.

We'll help any way we can.

I know, thanks!! Btw, is Amanda okay? It seemed like she wanted her space or whatever, so I haven't wanted to bother her.

I don't know. She's been doing stuff this weekend with her friend Stephanie, and I don't want to get in the way. I got the cupcake like Angelina said, but Amanda wasn't home when I went to bring it to her house after dinner Friday. I'll make sure she got it when I see her in school tomorrow.

I'm sure she wouldn't think you're in the way. You're one of her best friends.

I know. But Stephanie is her oldest best friend besides Leo of course. Like Annabelle is mine, and Bailey is yours. No matter how much you lose touch or grow apart as you get older and make new friends, no one will ever know you like the friends you had when you were little. Don't forget about them. That's your lecture of the day. :0)

It's a good one. I'm going to go give Bailey a call! XO

XO. Thank you again for what you did.

Aw shucks, it was nothing. :P

TARA

Dear Julie,

Uncle Roger has the BEST surprise for my friend Connor in the history of surprises. Remember, Connor's the one who works for my uncle after school sometimes since he wants to be an inventor when he grows up? Well, he didn't want to wait that long, so he's been working on a super-secret project (actually, it's a pair of 3-D glasses that people who wear glasses can comfortably wear). I know this because David is working on it with him as his beta tester (that's someone who tests devices in early stages), and David told me. He and I agreed not to keep secrets from each other. ANYWAY, Connor showed my uncle his prototype (that's like a sample, sorry if I keep explaining all the inventor lingo!), and my uncle thought it was great!

He suggested a few ways to tweak it, like offering a version that snaps onto your real glasses, and now he's going to help Connor find an investor (that's someone who puts money behind a product to help it get started)! But the surprise is that while Connor was in school the other day, Uncle Roger hired a company to make fifty samples based exactly on the prototype, so that people can start wearing them, and then buzz will build around them! (Buzz is like gossip, but the good kind! Like when people are all talking about something new, and then everyone wants one!)

So that's the big news here! Do you have plans for Halloween? I haven't dressed up since I was nine, but apparently in Willow Falls it's a big deal, so I have to come up with an outfit.

w/b/s

Tara

PS: I'm sorry about dumping all that stuff on you in the last letter. I feel much better. It's amazing the power of the pool hole! I can go there anytime I need a break from life. I think I will be okay.

PPS: One more thing . . . it turns out I'm a writer and didn't even know it! Guess you might have suspected it after you got that huge box of letters a few months ago, but I never thought of myself that way. My dad said he would help me try to get a story published some day! And that we

could try to write a book together! Me = didn't think I
was good at anything special. I'm enclosing a photocopy
of my first story *The Day Tara the Great Destroyed the
Zombie Queen and Then Ate a Grilled Cheese Sandwich*.
Try not to laugh, since I wrote it a long time ago! I hope
you like it!

PPPS: Loved the picture of your adorable dog Rapunzel!
I didn't expect her to be a black lab with such short hair!
Thank you for explaining what *irony* means, because I
never really got that till now!

Chapter Thirteen

GRACE

I plop down on the front lawn. Five more minutes to go. I've had to wait a week for the others all to be free at the same time. Amanda's been busy with marching band, Tara started taking fencing lessons, and Leo's friend Vinnie convinced him to try out for soccer. Basically they've all been leading these totally normal lives, while I've been going to school during the day, then staring into the window of Angelina's store the rest of the afternoon trying to figure out where half of everything went. Getting inside must have been a one-time deal, because the key no longer works.

I didn't tell any of them about the stuff disappearing, or how panicked I am about finding the vortex. They may have promised to look out for me, but I can't expect them to drop everything all the time. Bailey's the one person I can confide everything in. I know she's not going anywhere. Even though she obviously hadn't been camping with Leo, Amanda, Ray, Tara, and Rory the night they learned about the vortex, Bailey would have been here if her mom hadn't surprised her with tickets to a charity fashion show in River Bend. I couldn't let her turn down something like that. Connor and David weren't there that night, either, and even though they offered to come with me, too, I knew they'd have more fun working on Connor's secret invention (which everyone seems to know about but me, so maybe it's not that secret after all).

My hand drifts up to the spot above my ear. Little tufts are just starting to grow in the bald spot. I hope my sunglasses came in handy after sacrificing a clump of hair for them!

Leo arrives first, then Amanda, then Ray and Tara pull up in Ray's car, leaving only Rory still missing.

"Do you think Rory's seen the picture yet?" Tara asks as soon as she's hopped out of the car.

Before I can ask what picture, Amanda says, "I don't think so. We'd have heard the screams of horror."

"Remember, this is Rory we're talking about," Leo says. "She's survived much worse embarrassment than this."

"True," Amanda says, "but that's when people didn't notice her. Now she's dating a movie star."

"Sort of dating," Tara corrects her. "Not officially until she's older. Remember her dad made Jake sign something?"

I thought that was only a rumor, but the ins and outs of teen romance aren't something I can really relate to.

"Anyway," Amanda continues, "hopefully it'll blow over and she won't find out." I notice she and Leo aren't quite meeting each other's eyes when they talk to the group.

"Sorry I'm late," Rory says, breathless. She drops her bike on the grass and joins our circle. "It's been a crazy morning. So I don't know if Grace told any of you guys about how we had to wear these pointy tinfoil hats last weekend?"

Everyone acts like they didn't hear her. Teenagers are strange.

"Maybe this will refresh your memories," Rory says, and pulls her hat out of her bike basket. She sticks it on her head and says, "So my mom took a picture of me wearing it because she thought it was really funny. Then this morning Sawyer was playing with our mom's phone and somehow, I'm still not sure how, he accidentally uploaded the picture to the Internet! I can't find my phone — I know, don't say it! — so I haven't been able to check where it went. Hopefully no one saw it!"

Ray starts whistling, Amanda picks at the grass, Tara ties her sneaker, and Leo asks, "Does that cloud look like a moose to anyone else?"

Finally Ray says, "Someone's gotta tell her."

"Tell me what?" Rory asks.

Amanda and Tara exchange a look. Tara gives a slight nod. Amanda pulls out her phone and reluctantly hands it to Rory.

"Ugh, are you kidding me?" Rory says, slapping her forehead. "This isn't even the one my mom took!"

I peek over her shoulder. It's a picture of her in the tinfoil hat coming out of the diner. She's holding a white box just big enough for a cupcake. The heading on the photo reads, *Jake Harrison's "charity project" has strange fashion sense!*

Rory lays her head down in Amanda's lap. "There, there," Amanda says, stroking Rory's hair. "I bet you just started a trend. By next week all the cool kids will want a hat like yours!"

Rory just whimpers. Then she suddenly stops and sits up. "Hey! Soon no one will pay any attention to me again! Grace used her magic to make Jake look like an ordinary kid when he's out in public. So the next time the paparazzi stalk me, they'll see me with some random dude and think we broke up! I'll be free to do embarrassing things again and no one will care!"

The others cheer and pat me on the back.

I hold up my hand. "All right, all right. Any of you would have done the same. Now let's talk vortex!"

Leo doesn't have his mallet, so he just thumps his fist on the ground and says, "An official meeting of Team Grace — minus David, Connor, and Bailey — is now called to order. First on the agenda is to help Grace find the vortex so she can fully restore her powers." He turns to me. "That's right, isn't it?"

I nod.

He continues. "So as chairman, I ask that each of you take a moment to think back to the night of the campout at Apple Grove. What did Bucky tell us about the vortex?"

"I remember he said it wasn't too far from where we were sitting at the time, right?" Tara asks. "Around the campfire?"

Amanda agrees. Rory sits up and nods, too.

Leo turns to Ray. "Do you remember anything else?"

Ray shakes his head. "It was a long conversation. I had to fight to stay awake!"

"Well, then," Leo says, "I guess that's all we have to go on. Sorry, Grace, I know it's not much."

"That's okay. I thought maybe if you guys were all together, it would spark a memory."

"It sparks a lot of memories," Amanda says quietly. "That was a really great night."

The others nod. "Yes, it was," Leo says, daring to look at Amanda full-on for the first time this morning.

I grab the dowsing rods from the ground beside me and stand. "At least we know where to start. That's a lot."

We pile into Ray's car and head toward Apple Grove. When we get onto Main Street Tara says, "Emily loved the giraffe. Thanks, Grace!"

"About that night at the store . . ." I begin. "There's something I should tell you guys."

Ray slows the car. "I don't like the sound of that. You're not going to tell me those golf clubs I took are haunted by some evil spirit and I'll lose every round?"

"Nope. If you lose it's all on you. But after we left the store that night, I saw that half the stuff inside was gone."

"Did we take too much?" Tara asks, sounding worried. "I can put back that magnetic chess set I snagged at the last second. I don't even play chess!"

"No, no, it's not what you guys took. The store itself, it . . . *changed.*"

From the front seat, Amanda gasps and whirls her head

around to face the backseat. Ray gets startled by her sudden moves and screeches to a halt. Fortunately, there's no one behind us.

"Holy dooly!" he says to her. "Are you all right?"

"Sorry!" she says. "But I can't believe I forgot to tell you guys! You know the watch store on the corner when you first turn into the alley?"

"Yeah," we all say.

"It's gone!" she says.

"You mean, it closed?" Rory asks. "Not that big a surprise."

"It's more gone than that," Amanda says. "Like, gone gone."

"We're only a block away," Ray says. "Might as well have a lookie-lu." He pulls into a spot in front of the toy store and we all climb out.

Leo falls into step beside Amanda as we head to the alley. "You just forgot to tell us? That seems like a strange thing to forget."

"I know," Amanda says, but doesn't explain further.

We all turn the corner together and gape. Gone gone is right! I was half expecting to see an out-of-business sign tacked up on the door. But the entire building is gone, like it never existed. When did this happen? "How have I walked by it all week without noticing?" I ask.

"Don't feel too bad," Rory says. "That's how it can be with the magic in Willow Falls. If you're not looking for it, you usually don't notice."

"Then why did Amanda see it?" Leo asks.

"Out of all of Team Grace, she's the most sensitive to magic," Rory says. "Haven't you noticed? That's why she knew I'd met Angelina last year, and when Tara had, too. Right, Amanda?"

Amanda nods in agreement, still staring at the alley. She's been more quiet than usual recently, so I don't want to make her more uncomfortable by putting her on the spot.

"C'mon, guys," I say, pulling them away. "I'll show you the store, then we should really go."

They follow me down the narrow alley. The shoe-repair store and barbershop are still here, empty as always. Leo begins to drag his feet. "Um, does anyone else feel like the walls are kind of closing in?"

We slow and look around. "The alley does seem kind of narrower," Tara says.

Now that she mentions it, the stores do seem closer to one another than before. There's barely room for us all to walk side by side now.

"This is super creepy," Ray says. "Let's hurry and get out before we're turned into pancakes!"

"Mmmm, pancakes," Leo says, rubbing his belly.

Rory grabs him by the sleeve and drags him along.

"See?" I say, pointing in the store window. Then it's my turn to gasp. It's even emptier than it was before! Much more!

"Wow!" Tara says, her eyes wide. "Where did everything go?"

I can only shake my head.

"Did someone break in?" Ray asks, trying the knob. It's as locked as ever.

"No offense," Leo says, "but who would want this stuff? It's mostly junk, right?"

"'It will open doors to wonders unimagined,'" I whisper.

"Huh?" he says.

"That's what Angelina told me in the letter she left for me with the key."

He shakes his head. "Guess I can't see it."

I want to argue that all this stuff meant something to someone once, but it's no use. Most of it's gone now, anyway. But where? And why? And how?

Amanda shivers. "Let's get to Apple Grove before anything else weird happens, okay?"

"Race you to the car," Ray says, and we all take off at a run.

. . . .

Ten minutes later we're hiking up the path to Apple Grove. The baby trees are only slightly larger than the last time I was here, the morning of David's bar mitzvah, the morning my life changed forever.

Amanda and Leo give the trees loving pats as we pass by, occasionally stopping to straighten one out or push some more soil around the base. The fountain in the middle is in better shape than I remember. They must have done some work on it.

I follow them to the fire pit and pull out the dowsing rods.

"Do you know how to use those?" Tara asks.

"I was reading up on it," I tell her as I adjust my grip on the handles. "First, I need to know what direction I'm facing."

"That's easy," Leo says. "There's a compass on the edge of the fountain, see?" He points to a metal plate attached to the rim of the bowl. "Right now you're facing south."

"Thanks. Okay, so then basically I hold them out like this, parallel to the ground, and they swivel around in my hands when I move. They're supposed to straighten out when I'm heading in the right direction. Then, when I reach the energy source — in this case, the vortex — they're supposed to stretch open wide in both directions."

"That's a lot of 'supposed to's,'" Ray says.

"Way to boost her confidence!" Tara scolds.

Ray holds up his hands. "Don't get your knickers in a knot, I was just kidding."

Tara tries to kick him, but he jumps back.

"You said the rods can find things other than energy centers, right?" Leo asks. "Like oil, or water, or gold?"

I nod.

"Well, if you don't find the vortex, maybe focus on the gold. Buried pirate gold!"

"There aren't any pirates in Willow Falls," Amanda says.

"Sure," he says, "not now, but maybe the town was closer to water once. There was that river! At least until your great-great-great-grandfather dammed it up."

The corners of her mouth quiver and I can tell she's trying not to smile. "It was YOUR great-great-great-grandfather who dammed up the river!"

"Oh. You sure?"

"Um, guys?" Rory says. "Can we focus, please?"

"Sorry," Amanda says.

"Sorry," Leo mutters.

I take a deep breath and close my eyes. "Vortex of

power," I whisper to the rods. "Guide me to the vortex of power."

I open my eyes and in slow, measured steps begin to move forward. The rods sway gently back and forth along with my movements but don't straighten out. I turn west and try again. They don't begin to straighten out until I turn north.

Leo begins to laugh. All the girls shush him.

"Sorry!" he says. "It's just that you're facing the mall now. What if the vortex is inside the Gap! Or, wait, I bet it's in the food court! The vortex could be inside Panda Pavilion!"

"A panda would make a fine spirit animal," Ray says cheerfully.

"Hush!" Rory says. "The vortex isn't in the food court!"

"You're probably right," Leo says, turning serious. Then he blurts out, "I bet it's in the underwear department at Macy's!"

This time, when Tara kicks, she doesn't miss. Leo yelps.

I'm sure the vortex is not in the mall, but still I'm relieved when I walk a few steps north and the rods swing to the right. I quickly turn east and walk forward. The rods immediately straighten out. I look like Frankenstein's monster, with the rods sticking straight out in front of me like really skinny arms. The others shout and gather around.

I take another deep breath, focus my thoughts again, and begin to walk. It only takes a minute before we enter the woods. There's no path, but the trees, a mix of evergreen, birch, and elm, are wide enough apart that it's easy to pass through them. The ground slopes gently upward, and we follow it.

"Hey," Leo says. "This is near where Amanda's and my ancestors lived. When we went back in time and saw them as little kids, this was the direction they came from."

"And I think the road that leads to Angelina's house is on the other side of these woods, too," Tara says. "We've just never approached it from this side before."

"Sounds like a good place for a vortex to me!" Rory says.

It's beginning to feel like the dowsing rods are pulling me now instead of leading me. The tug gets stronger and stronger until I'm stumbling after them.

"Anyone else notice the smell?" Amanda asks.

The second she mentions it, the smell hits me and everyone else at the same time. Apples! This isn't the usual the-air-smells-like-apples-when-magic-is-around kind of thing, this is for real. We look around as we continue hurling ourselves forward. There haven't been apple trees here in decades. Where is the smell coming from?

A minute later, we burst through the trees and stumble into a small clearing that I'd never have guessed was up here. The dowsing rods spread wide open, like they're opening their arms to embrace a welcome guest. We have arrived.

Chapter Fourteen

GRACE

The six of us stand in a row and stare at the lone tree in the center of the clearing. The surprising part isn't that it's an apple tree, but rather that it's got to be the strangest apple tree that ever existed anywhere on the planet. Ever.

For one thing, its branches, which start about ten feet above the ground, don't extend outward in all directions like you'd expect. Instead, they curl around the trunk, like the tree knows some big secret and is hugging itself to contain it.

As twisted as the branches are, they are still dripping with apples. Ripe, red, full, juicy apples. The source of the smell, for sure. The power here thumps through the ground. I can actually feel it pulsing through me. I look at the others and know they feel it, too. Not as strongly as I do, but they feel it.

"What do you do now?" Rory asks, resting her hand on my arm.

The rods swing back to their neutral position. I kneel and rest them on a flat rock at my feet. "I'm not sure," I admit. I hadn't planned that far ahead.

As I stand back up, I notice there are a lot of rocks around the size of my foot, most of them covered over with grass. I also spot an old stone bench on the outskirts of the clearing, mostly hidden by overgrown brush. I point at the ground. "What do you think the story is with these rocks? They don't look like they were placed here randomly."

We begin kicking aside grass and dirt with our shoes, following different paths of rock. "It's like a big circle," Leo says.

"Circles inside circles," Tara adds. "But some of the stones are missing. There are big gaps."

I stop short. The pattern reminds me of something. I pull the pouch out of my back pocket and find Angelina's first postcard. *Greetings from . . . Stonehenge!* shouts up at me.

Stonehenge. It literally means *stone circle.*

I flip the card over. The symbols of my friends swim before my eyes. One circle inside another, inside another.

"It's a labyrinth," I announce. "And we're supposed to rebuild it."

Standing here, in the shadow of the vortex, everyone can clearly see the writing on the card now. No one questions my conclusion.

We fan out and run back into the woods to find more stones to match the others. Ray gets busy clearing off the stones that are already there. We start out very focused on our task, but then start getting silly. We dart in and out of one another's paths, hiding behind trees and scaring one another when we pass. Tara has so many rocks in her arms I don't know how she moves!

Eventually we have enough and start filling in the gaps. Now that we can clearly see the old ones, it's pretty easy to follow the circular lines. Whether on purpose or not, everyone leaves the innermost circle for me to fill in. I'm not sure they're comfortable being so close to the vortex. Even I don't want to get too close to the tree. What if it sucks me in and spins me around for all eternity? I shudder. From a few feet away I can see markings on the surprisingly smooth trunk. I can't tell if they're natural or man-made, but a closer inspection will have to wait.

When we're done, we step back to admire our handiwork.

"We've got some serious labyrinth-building skills," Leo says, wiping his hands together to dislodge the dirt. I've already wiped mine all over my clothes. Mom will be thrilled.

"Totally!" Rory says. "We could make this our career! People would hire us from all over the —"

But she doesn't get to finish. At that moment, a wave of energy, stronger than the one I felt in the store last week, bursts out of the tree and knocks us all off our feet.

"Is everyone all right?" Ray asks, crawling over. We groan and sit up. "Everyone say *aye* if you're okay."

"Aye," we each say in turn.

"Aye aye, matey," Leo says, doing his best pirate imitation.

"That was crazy," Tara says, rubbing her elbows. "What happened?"

"I felt it once before," I tell them. "Last Friday night in the store. It almost knocked me over then, too. But Tara and Ray didn't feel anything."

"I felt it last Friday night, too," Amanda says quietly. We all turn to look at her. "It was near the end of the gymnastics meet. So maybe around eight fifteen-ish?"

"That's when I felt the one in the store," I tell her.

"I figured I'd just imagined it," Amanda says, "but then I couldn't shake the feeling that something was different.

And then on the way home is when I saw the watch store had gone. I'm sorry I didn't say something sooner, about either of those things. It's almost like I forgot it, like I dreamed it."

"I totally get it," I assure her. "It's like that for me sometimes, too."

She smiles at me gratefully.

"But what *was* it?" Tara asks. "If the last wave can be connected with the things changing in the alley — which it definitely sounds like it was — then what happened this time? Is the entire alley gone now?"

None of us have an answer to that.

"Look," Rory says, pointing up at the sky. "Even Max and Flo felt it."

The two hawks are circling the vortex, one gliding behind the other. Flo lets out a high-pitched *kreeee*, Max makes a sound like *garuuuunk*. They make one more circle, then soar off in opposite directions. We turn our heads to follow Flo, then Max, then back to Flo as if we're watching a tennis match. My heart starts pounding harder and harder the farther apart they get. Soon we can no longer spot their yellow feet against the blue sky.

"I . . . I don't understand," Rory says, visibly shaken. "I've never seen those birds more than a few feet apart in my entire life."

"Me, neither," Amanda and Leo echo.

Max and Flo have been residents of Willow Falls since before any of us were born. I couldn't believe it when, over the summer, Tara told me they were actually under a twenty-five-year-old love spell!

"What does this mean?" Tara asks now. They all look to me for the answer.

I close my eyes and try to let the threads of recent events knit together. My eyes snap open. "The magic in Willow Falls is unraveling!"

"What??" the girls shout, grabbing my arms.

"The vortex is undoing all the work Angelina did!" I tell them, beginning to pace in a circle. "Anything magical is slowly disappearing. Like the alley, we always knew there was something enchanted about it. I've never seen anyone besides us walk down it, have you guys?"

They all shake their heads. Leo says, "David said he went into the watch store once with his grandfather when he was a little kid. I remember he said it smelled like feet."

"Why would a watch store smell like feet?" Ray asks.

"He could have been confusing it with someplace else," Leo says.

"Either way," I continue, "there was always something weird about that street and we've seen with our own eyes what's been happening there. And now the spell that bound Max and Flo forever is broken! After being each other's constant companions for a quarter of a century, they're flying in different directions."

"Probably a bit relieved," Ray says under his breath. Tara kicks him. Maybe she should try out for soccer instead of fencing.

"It takes magic to undo magic," Amanda says firmly. "Someone is undoing it."

Chapter Fourteen and a Half

In a house across town . . .

Sylvia Johnston knew immediately that something was wrong. It wasn't only the horrified stares of the women in her knitting circle, or the tingles across her cheeks and down her chin. She could actually *see* the shadows of the warts out of the corners of her eyes. Her eyes widened, her vision blurred, but she was not imagining it. After all these years, the warts the doctors had claimed were incurable were back.

And they were *angry*.

"Sylvia!" her oldest and dearest friend, Ruth Ann, shouted, clutching her ball of yarn to her chest. "Your face! Your beautiful face!"

Sylvia jumped up, knocking her own yarn and half-made scarf onto the rug. She ran to the mirror to verify what she already knew. Angelina D'Angelo had cured her decades ago, asking nothing in return but her silence. She'd given it willingly and always made certain to look Angelina in the eye and smile when she passed her in town, while many others turned their heads away.

Sylvia's friends gathered around her, saying supportive things like "Don't worry, you can hardly see them" and "With modern medicine you'll be able to clear those right up" and "Milt's eyes are so bad he won't even notice them." When Sylvia just continued to stare at her reflection, turning her face left and right, Lucille chimed in with "Vanity is a young woman's folly. Who cares how you look on the outside?" But they all knew it wasn't as simple as that.

Sylvia plopped back down on the sofa while Ruth Ann hurried to call the pharmacist. Sylvia knew she wasn't the only one Angelina had helped over the years, far from it. She closed her eyes and said a little prayer that her warts returning would keep the others from suffering a more serious reversal of fortune. Then she let Ruth Ann tie a scarf around her face and lead her to the door.

Chapter Fifteen

GRACE

"You don't think Angelina's behind the magic unraveling," Tara asks, "do you?"

I shake my head. "I think she still has some power left, even if she's trying to hide it, but not nearly enough for something like this. Plus, she worked for a hundred years to protect this town, so no way is she going to undo all that."

"What about someone else?" Amanda asks.

"No one else can use the vortex's power," I tell them, sure of it. "Only me, Angelina, and whoever came before her. And that person would have passed her powers to Angelina, like Angelina passed them to me. It's in my DNA or something, so unless I have an unknown evil twin running around —"

"That's it!" Leo shouts.

"Grace doesn't have an evil twin!" Rory insists.

"Not that," Leo says. "What if someone took your DNA and can channel your powers that way? Like when you were in the hospital, did anyone take your blood?"

My eyes widen. "Yes, they took a ton those first few days. My parents wanted them to test for everything they could think of. You don't think someone stole it from the hospital, do you?"

"Can you think of any other time someone could have taken blood?" Tara asks.

"DNA is in your saliva, too," Ray points out.

"Did you spit on anyone recently?" Leo asks.

The thought of me spitting on someone and them keeping it is so absurd, I actually laugh.

Rory asks Tara if she can borrow her phone. "I'm going to call David," she says. "Since he wants to be a doctor, he reads a lot of stuff about DNA."

He picks up right away, and she asks him how someone could get your DNA if they wanted it. "You're with Connor and I don't want to worry him," she says in response to what was no doubt his questioning why she wanted to know. "I'll tell you later, I promise." She listens for a minute, then hangs up and hands Tara back the phone.

"Well, apparently almost every cell in your body has DNA in it," she reports. "You can get it from skin, blood, mucus, saliva, hair follicles, nails — hey, you didn't get a manicure recently, did you?"

My hand flies up to my head, to the spot where the hair came out with the glasses. The last thread weaves itself into place. I almost choke from trying to get the words out so fast. "It's Connor! He yanked some hair out when he took my giant sunglasses to use for his invention. The follicles must have gotten embedded in there somewhere!"

"That's totally it!" Leo shouts. "Connor's been looking through those glasses to test them out. I bet Tara's uncle has used them, too, and David."

"But what's he using them for?" I ask. "He still hasn't told me."

"He's making frames to attach to people's glasses to watch 3-D movies more comfortably," Tara says. "Family's always the last to know, I guess!"

"But how is that affecting the magic in town?" I ask.

"I'm no rocket scientist," Ray says, "but it seems to me, when your brother's brain is using the glasses to decode a 3-D signal, he is using your DNA at the same time. But since it's combined with *his* DNA, the vortex is flipping out and randomly undoing the magic. This is fun! Like a detective show on the telly!"

Leo begins to pace. "If it happens to us, Amanda and I would be stuck in our birthday again!"

"Not only that," Rory says. "David's grandfather will disappear, his dad will be sick again, and so will David one day."

I look at Tara, who has gone pale. Her whole life would unravel, too, not to mention all the countless other people whose lives have been touched by the vortex's magic that I'd never even know about.

"Okay, let's not panic," I tell them. "We can solve this. We'll call Connor and David and tell them not to use the glasses again. I'll take them and keep them safe. I'm kind of afraid to destroy them, just in case they're linked to me somehow."

Amanda and Leo reach for their phones to make the call.

Tara shakes her head. "It won't work," she says. "It's not just the one pair now."

"What do you mean?" I ask.

"It was going to be a surprise for your brother. Uncle Roger used Connor's prototype to get fifty samples made. He copied it exactly. *Exactly*. Down to the chemical composition in the frames. He's already sent out a bunch to people in the TV industry who he knows. He thinks this could be huge for home theatres, too."

We all stare at her as this sinks in. My DNA will be in ALL of the glasses! There will be no way to control the effect on the vortex. One by one the threads that bind this town together, that bind *us* together, will unfurl and break.

"I have to shut down the vortex," I announce.

"You can't," Rory says. "You'll lose your powers. What about your destiny?"

"Maybe *this* is my destiny," I reply. "To be the one to shut it down. This way the energy can flow somewhere else where it's needed."

"But, Grace," Amanda says, "won't shutting it down just undo everything all at once?"

"I . . . I don't know," I admit. "I don't think so. But at least this gives us a chance at saving what we can. Will you help me?"

They exchange looks, then nod.

I turn to Leo and Ray. "Will you guys watch from outside the labyrinth and make sure nothing goes wrong? If you see me getting sucked into the vortex, rush in!"

"You better be kidding about that last part," Ray says. "Your parents expect you home in one piece, little lady."

"I'll do my best." I wave for the girls to follow me. Amanda runs over to Leo. I see her shove something blue into his hand. "This reminded me of your eyes," she whispers, louder than she probably intended to. Before he can answer, she turns and joins me and Tara and Rory at the entrance of the labyrinth. I knew I would need them for something big one day, and that day is upon us.

I'm tempted to run straight to the tree in the center, but that's not what a labyrinth is for. So we start at the entrance and march along Tara's outer circle. The labyrinth curves, and we're in Rory's circle, then Amanda's. Finally, the four of us stand in the middle, in front of the tree.

"What now?" Tara asks.

"I don't know," I admit. "We need to connect to it somehow." I kick off my sneakers and peel off my socks. The others do the same. I dig my feet into the soil, trying to ground myself in the earth. The others follow. The pulsing beat of the vortex now matches my own. I imagine a beam of energy entering through the top of my head, reaching deep into the source of the vortex's power.

Then I ask it, out loud, very politely, to shut itself down.

It doesn't.

I'm definitely connected to it, though, because I can feel that another wave is about to hit. "Duck!" I shout. We duck and hold on to one another as the wave bursts forth. It's easier to handle when prepared. This time we're just a little windblown.

"Um, Grace?" Rory tugs on my sleeve. "You're shorter."

"What?"

"You've shrunk, like, an inch," Amanda says, her voice shaking. "The magic is still coming undone."

"Okay," I say as bravely as possible. "I can live with losing an inch. Let's hope everyone else was spared."

"Why didn't it stop when you asked?" Rory asks.

"Maybe because you forgot this," Ray shouts from where he and Leo are standing on the stone bench. *"Again."*

It's the bag of seeds!

"Catch!" he says, and lobs it overhand. I watch as the bag sails through the labyrinth, almost in slow motion. Tara reaches up and catches it neatly with one hand.

"Here ya go," she says.

"Maybe baseball instead of fencing?" Rory suggests.

I pull on the ribbon and the top of the bag opens. Without thinking of what I'm supposed to do, I reach in and grab a handful of seeds. I sprinkle them all over the ground around the tree. "Oh, powerful vortex," I say, feeling a little silly. "I am grateful for all the bounty you have given me and the whole town for so long." I turn over the bag and let the last few seeds drift to the ground. "But we really, really need you to stop now."

"Well," Rory says, after a moment. "That oughta do it!"

We watch the tree, barely daring to breathe.

Stubbornly, the tree just keeps pulsing with energy. Fear sends icy spikes up my back. *What if I can't make the vortex stop?*

Tara moves first. "What are these marks?" she asks, stepping closer to the tree. She traces them with her finger. "It looks like someone carved pictures into the trunk."

The rest of us inch a little closer. "They're animals!" Amanda exclaims. "Look, here's an owl, here's a duck . . . I'm not sure what this one is."

"It's a bunny," Rory says grimly.

"These are spirit animals!" Tara says.

"I told you so!" Ray shouts over to us.

We ignore him.

"Each of them must be from someone who could control the vortex," Tara says. "I bet we all know who the duck was!"

"Angelina!" we cry out at the same time.

"What's yours, Grace?" Rory asks.

I look at Tara, and out at Ray. "I . . . I still don't know."

"It's a lion," Amanda says so quietly I almost don't hear her.

"What did you say?" Rory asks.

"Grace's spirit animal is a lion," Amanda says, louder this time.

"How do you know that?" I ask.

She reaches into her pocket and pulls out a yellow plastic lion with what looks like a toothpick stuck in the bottom of it.

"It's the cupcake topper from the cupcake Rory brought me," she says.

"There was a lion on a SpongeBob cupcake?" I ask.

She nods. "I figured it must have gotten mixed up with the one next to it."

"I didn't even notice when I bought the cupcake," Rory says. "Why did you keep it? Why did you bring it?"

She glances over at the bench where Ray and Leo are, then says, "It's kind of embarrassing. I collect things that remind me of Leo. You know, Leo the lion. The astrology sign?"

Amanda allows herself a peek at Leo, who is listening intently, his hands grasped together. She quickly looks back at me. "But, Grace, the lion wasn't about Leo, it was about you."

"How can you be sure?" I ask. "If I carve the wrong animal in the trunk, who knows what might happen."

"I'm sure," she says firmly. "Angelina told you guys to get me that cupcake, right?"

Rory and I exchange a look of surprise. "How did you know?" she asks.

"Come on, that move has Angelina written all over it. A SpongeBob cupcake when I needed to be reminded of what me and Leo mean to each other? And it just *happens* to have a random lion cupcake topper on it when you need to find a spirit animal, one that represents courage, strength, and power more than any other?"

"She's right," Tara says. "That would be too much of a coincidence. Do I even need to say it?"

I shake my head. "I know, I know. There are no coincidences in Willow Falls."

"That's the truth, sistah," Tara says, bending down to pick up a pointy stick. "Now get carving."

I do my best, but when I'm done the lion looks more like a fluffy kitten than a fierce king of the jungle. Hopefully it's good enough. I lay the stick back down.

Amanda puts out her hand and I take it. Then I reach for Rory's, and Rory reaches for Tara's. Tara takes Amanda's and the circle around the tree is complete.

"Brace yourselves," I say. We all dig our feet back into the earth again and close our eyes. I focus on feeling like a lion, and wait until I actually feel the strength and courage of him within me. Then I thrust him out of me, and into the tree. I open my eyes. The carving no longer looks like a kitten. There's no doubt now what it is. The others still have their eyes closed, unaware that I've set things in motion. Or at least I hope I have.

At first, nothing happens. Then it happens all at once. The wind howls as branches begin to unfurl themselves, slowly at first, then picking up speed, whipping over our heads. Our hair flies around our faces, but we don't let go of one another's hands. I see Ray and Leo jumping around in alarm, but they don't dare get too close.

Apples fly off the branches in all directions, flinging themselves at our feet, bouncing off stones, filling the pathways of the labyrinth. I blink, and the tree is no longer a tree. It's a swirling tunnel of pure energy, pure possibility. I can see inside it, to the calm part in the very center. In there lies the building blocks of the whole universe.

Energy waits to become matter, it waits for our choices to make reality solid. I finally understand what Angelina meant with her physics lesson. Everything is real, and nothing is real. This brings me a great sense of peace. As my connection to the vortex weakens, my body is filled with its own energy, and it shines out of every cell. This is the glow I see when I look at my friends and family. What I've always seen, if I only knew to look. This energy links us together, it binds us and protects us. It reminds us we are a part of a greater whole.

I feel a surge of gratitude and love for the brave girls beside me. I'm surprised to see their eyes are still shut, their faces a range of emotions. I squeeze their hands, and suddenly I'm where they are, seeing what they see, feeling what they feel. They are not here. They are in their futures, *our* futures.

The vortex is feeding them a great gift as its power quickly drains. The last few branches of the apple tree snap into place. The pulsing in the ground slows to a dull thump, and then to nothing at all. Somewhere, the energy is already building beneath a new town, where someone else will be chosen to wield it.

And me? I'm just a regular girl now, standing in front of a regular tree, in a regular little town. But I have glimpsed the true nature of reality. Someday I'll learn more, and I'll share it. People will listen.

And they'll understand they are part of something amazing.

RORY AT THE VORTEX

One minute I'm holding my friends' hands in the labyrinth, the next I'm on a sunny football field. But not a real one, it's a movie set. I can tell because there are lights and boom microphones and people running around yelling "cut" and "send in the extras." A group of actors in football uniforms are getting direction by a man in a backward baseball cap. I'm standing behind a row of sound equipment, so I can watch the scene being filmed without getting in the way. Jake must be one of the actors on the field! Otherwise, why would I be on a film set?

I glance around and find an empty chair with the words DIRECTOR — JAKE HARRISON printed on the back. I back away in surprise, then grin. He did it! He followed his dream and became a director!

A few seconds later, the group of actors breaks up, and the man in the baseball hat heads to the chair. He looks over at me and gives me a big grin and a thumbs-up before sitting down.

My heart flips over. It's Jake, but he's grown up! At least thirty or thirty-five, I can't tell ages of old people. If he's grown up, I must be, too. I glance down at my hands. I don't register if they look older or not because I am mesmerized by the diamond ring and gold wedding band on my left hand.

Now my heart is really racing! We're together! We're married!!

"Action!" Jake shouts. The crowd immediately hushes up.

I catch my breath as a little boy, around four or five, runs across the field in an oversized football jersey that says PIRATES on it. At first I think it's Sawyer. But it can't be. If I'm grown up, he would be, too. As the boy gets closer, I can see he's wearing an eye patch! I have to put my hand over my mouth to keep from laughing. The boy stops in front of the largest camera and says, "Go, Pirates!" The football players cheer and race onto the field.

"Cut!" Jake calls. "Print! Great job, everyone!"

The little boy beams, sees me, and starts running over. As he passes Jake, the two of them high-five, then the boy runs right into my arms. He's beautiful.

"Mom!" the boy shouts up at me. "Guess what? Uncle Jake said I could keep my eye patch! Now I can be a pirate for Halloween!"

My heart speeds up. I'm a MOM! Uncle Jake? He said Uncle Jake! The boy breaks away from me and races toward a man in jeans and a T-shirt whose face I can't see from this angle. "Dad!" he shouts. "Did you see my scene?"

The man says, "Of course, buddy! You were awesome!" He swings the boy up onto his shoulders and parades him around the set. I look down at my finger. This is the man who has my heart now, there's no doubt. I feel a surge of love so powerful, it almost knocks me off my feet.

I look back over at Jake. He's deep in discussion with a woman holding out a movie script. The scene begins to fade away. I try to reach out for something to hold on to, something to keep me grounded here, but all I feel are hands in mine. I look down, hoping it's the boy's hands, or the man's, but they are gone.

I open my eyes. Tara and Amanda still have theirs closed, but Grace doesn't. She beams at me, her face streaked with tears and dirt, her hair wild around her. She squeezes my hand, and I squeeze back, not daring to speak.

I blink fast, trying to focus. Something happened just

now, something besides the vortex shutting down. I'm sure of it, but whatever it was has slipped away like the memory of a story you heard once a long time ago.

But it was a good story. A really, really good story. I know that much at least.

TARA AT THE VORTEX

One minute I'm up to my ankles in dirt, then the next I'm seated in one of about five hundred gray folding chairs on a huge rolling lawn surrounded by immense white stone buildings. I'm in a light-blue dress and heels. Heels? *Am I back at David's bar mitzvah in the dress I borrowed from Amanda's sister? But no, that doesn't make sense. There's no way this place is in Willow Falls.*

I look down at my lap. Resting there is a white booklet that reads: MEDICAL SCHOOL GRADUATION CEREMONY.

"Isn't this exciting?" a woman's voice asks beside me. I turn toward her so quickly I get dizzy. It's Grace! But she's all grown up! At least twenty-two. That must mean I'm older than that! Her red hair isn't quite as bright as when we were kids, and it's shorter, but her eyes are sparkling and full of life.

"The Hamburglar has worked so hard for this," a man says on the other side of Grace. Wait, it's not a man, it's Connor! Who I guess is a man now! He's dressed more casually than everyone, in jeans and a button-down shirt. Pretty much the same outfit Uncle Roger used to wear every day, since he worked at home. "But no one knows that better than you, Tara, right?"

I force myself to smile, even though I have no idea what he's talking about.

Grace puts her hand on mine. "I know it was rough there back in college, with you and David not being together for a while, and your dad getting sick, but I'm so glad you all pulled through it. You two belong together."

My heart starts thumping. I know she said something about me and David, but all I can think is, My dad was sick? Will be sick? Is still sick? Is . . . not here anymore?

"My dad?" I squeak out.

"There they are!" Connor says. He stands up and waves at a group of people looking for seats. "Mr. and Mrs. Goldberg! Mr. and Mrs. Brennan! Over here!"

I practically weep with relief to see my parents — older but very much alive. Dad is walking with a cane, but other than that he looks perfectly healthy and still just as tall.

They catch sight of us and start making their way through the crowd. I watch as a man in the audience stands up in front of my dad and says something to him. I can't hear what it is, though, but my dad nods and reaches into his pocket for something. His wallet maybe?

David's mom arrives at our seats first. She is still so beautiful, maybe more so. Her curly hair is still dark, and she only has a few more wrinkles than she did when I met her.

She laughs and says to me, "Since the TV series based on his last book came out, your dad can't go anywhere without signing autographs, Tara!"

So it wasn't his wallet he'd reached for, it was a pen!

"I bet you have that trouble, too!" she continues, squeezing my arm.

Me? Why would anyone want my autograph?

She sits down and beams at the three of us. "There must be something in the water in Willow Falls," she says. "Look at you all. One about to publish her fifth children's book, one starting graduate school in physics, and one award-winning inventor." She waves her booklet at the stage. "And my son, soon to be a doctor!"

My head begins to spin as they keep talking.

"Our other friends did pretty good for themselves, too," Connor says.

"Yeah," Grace says. "Remember my best friend, Bailey? She's a costume designer for movies now, in Hollywood! And Amanda Ellerby just opened a music school for kids."

Connor jumps in again. "Leo Fitzpatrick's on his way to becoming the youngest mayor in Willow Falls history! And Rory just got back from helping to build new schools in Africa. I heard she met a guy there."

"Really?" Grace asks, leaning forward. "What is he like?"

"How should I know?" Connor says, pinching his sister playfully on the arm. "Ask her yourself when they get here."

I'm getting dizzy from turning back and forth between them so quickly. I want to savor each bite, but each piece of information is coming so quickly. My parents and David's dad arrive next to take their seats. "David looks very handsome in his cap and gown," my mom says, pointing at the row of graduates who have started to file into the empty seats in the first few rows. "Very distinguished, don't you think?"

I scan the line, but at first I can't find him. Then I realize I'm looking for the thirteen-year-old version of him. I start searching from the front of the line again, but don't get too far before Connor and Grace start whooping and laughing. My mom gasps. Dad says, "Whoa!" Mr. Goldberg says, "That's my boy!"

Grace grabs my arm. "Finally!" she shouts.

"What do you mean?" I ask.

"Look!" She drags me to my feet and points at the graduates. The very last one is hanging back from the rest of the line a bit. He's wearing wire-rimmed glasses, and I can see David's dark hair peeking out from under the square graduation cap. And on the top of the cap are written five words.

"Tara, will you marry me?"

AMANDA AT THE VORTEX

First comes the smell, the overwhelming smell of apples on the breeze. For a minute, I think it must be coming from the vortex, but even though I can still feel my feet in the earth, I know I'm not in the circle anymore.

After the smell come the voices. Little voices, boys and girls. "Happy birthday to you! Happy birthday to you! Happy birthday, Grandpa and Grandma, happy birthday to you!"

Then someone fiddles with the back of my head and I realize they're untying a blindfold.

"Here we are, Mom and Dad," a woman's voice says. "What do you think?"

I blink as my eyes take in the scene. I'm still in Apple Grove, only it looks very, very different. The mall in the distance is now a gleaming white circular building. There's a large clearing in the middle of the grove with picnic tables and decorations. Our baby trees are fully grown, all but one now bearing ripe, red apples. An old man is standing beside me, blinking and beaming. He has kind, loving, mischievous eyes and a sprig of blue flowers pinned to his shirt. I realize with a jolt that it's Leo!

"You're so old!" I blurt out. My voice doesn't sound like mine. It sounds like my grandmother's!

Leo laughs. "If I'm old, what does that make you?"

The laughter spreads to the group of smiling faces around us. Faces I don't recognize, from middle-aged down to three or four. Wait, that woman's nose looks like my mom's nose. And that man's smile is exactly like Leo's. With another jolt it hits me that these people are my children and grandchildren! Leo is my husband! And we're old! REALLY old! Like, sixty-five!

Of course the big six-five spelled out in apples on the ground could have told me that, too!

I can't take my eyes away from Leo. He still has his curls, even though they're mostly white now.

"Wait till you see your gift," the same woman says. Our daughter! She has the same soft blond hair as my mom and Kylie have. Had? I look around, but don't see either of them.

The woman takes my hand. "The kids worked very hard on it," she says.

I look over at the group of kids. The littlest one presses a button on a small device in her hand and a holographic image appears a few feet away from us. I back up, startled, but Leo's hand is there to steady me. "Watch, Nana Mandy!" the little girl says. She can't be more than three.

In midair the word BIRTHDAYS appears. Then images slowly fade in and out. Many of them I recognize — there we are bowling at our sixth birthday party. There we are posing with the hypnotist at our eleventh. For our twelfth, we are standing in almost this exact spot, having just planted our first tree. Most of the images are totally unfamiliar, though. In one we are around fifteen or sixteen at the beach. In another we are a few years older, on a boat. I watch, open-jawed, as we grow up and grow old, together.

At the end, a short video plays. It's Leo and me as babies, at our first party. We're babbling and crawling, then almost at the same moment, stand and walk toward each other on wobbly legs. This moment is family lore in my house. I've never seen video of it before, though. They must have tracked it down from someone at the party. Or maybe I found it, sometime over the last few decades!

My daughter (!!) hands me a tissue. I hadn't realized tears

were pouring down my cheeks. "Are you all right, Mom?"
she asks.

*Leo turns away from our first steps and takes my hands
in his. I notice his eyes are misty, too. "Amanda Ellerby
Fitzpatrick, I will always keep walking toward you," he
says, kissing me on the forehead. He keeps his lips pressed
there, and I close my eyes as our family claps and hoots.
Relief pours through me. Sometimes your first love does
get to be your last.*

"Amanda," a boy's voice says. Then more urgently,
"Amanda!" Someone is tugging at my arm. I look down,
expecting it to be another grandchild. But it's Leo, and I'm
standing in the labyrinth and everyone is gathered around
me with concerned looks on their faces.

"Are you okay?" Leo asks. "You didn't open your eyes
for the longest time." He slides a leaf out of my hair.

I reach up to my forehead, feeling the ghost of a touch
pressed there. Then I blink, and it's gone. "Something
happened in the circle," I say. "Right?"

"Yes," Grace says. "We did it." She turns me around to
face the center. The tree! Its branches are straight, when
moments before they were wound tight around the trunk.
The apples that were hanging from its branches have been
flung all over the ground.

"Was there . . . something else, too?" I ask.

Grace doesn't answer.

"I think I went someplace," Rory says, stepping up beside me. She's absently rubbing her left hand.

"Me, too," Tara says, a faraway look in her eyes.

"Me, three," I say. I turn to Leo and really look at him for the first time in weeks. I reach for his hand. In front of everyone, I tell him the truest thing I know, although I don't know how I know it.

"Leo Fitzpatrick, I will always keep walking toward you."

Chapter Sixteen

GRACE

When I get back home, exhausted and exhilarated, Connor and David are waiting on the porch steps, a large cardboard box between them. They both stand up as I cross the lawn.

Seeing them like this — Connor's eyes twinkling, David healthy and carefree, with their whole futures in front of them — any lingering doubt I had over closing the vortex and giving up my powers drifts away for good.

Connor opens his mouth to greet me, but before the first words leave his mouth, I get a vision of his future. First come the 3-D glasses, then more gadgets, then he sets his sights on solving bigger problems. One day he's going to help figure out a way to turn everyday trash into fuel. It will cap a lifetime of making people's lives easier and better, in both small and large ways. I allow myself to watch him step up to a platform to accept an award. How proud our parents are!

"I have amazing news," Connor says, reaching into the box. "I wanted you to be the first person to have these."

Hearing his voice snaps me back to the present. I can still have visions! That's a surprise! Unable to help myself, I giggle. I think the vortex gave me a little gift, too.

I reach out and hug him. "I'm so proud of you, big brother." I can't tell him what I saw of his future, but there's no need. It will happen either way.

He untangles himself from my embrace. "I haven't even shown you yet." He hands me a pair of pink-framed tinted glasses and says, "I couldn't have done it without your help."

He doesn't know how true that is, just not in the way he thinks.

"Try them on," he urges. "David, give her your regular glasses to put on first."

David obliges and I slip them on. I was prepared for everything to look fuzzy, the way it does when I slip on my dad's glasses for fun. But I can see perfectly! "David! Your eyes must not be that bad at all. Nothing's even blurry!"

"Oh, right," he says. "That's because the lenses are just plain glass. I only wear them to make me look smarter. I got contacts over the summer."

Connor and I stare at him, shocked.

"Are you SERIOUS, dude?" Connor shouts, then starts cracking up. "This whole idea was because of you! And you didn't even need them? Man, that's messed up!"

I can only stare, my jaw hanging open. Everything we went through today was because Connor was inspired by David and his glasses. And now he won't even *need* them?

"Hey," David tells Connor, "believing I needed them got you to come up with your first invention, right? And this is just the beginning. One day you'll be huge."

He's right, of course. And I have to believe this was how it was supposed to happen. Maybe the vortex was ready to move on and it really was my destiny to help it.

I leave Connor still shaking his head at David and make my way into the house. I don't have the energy (literally) to tell them the story now. I'm sure David will hear all about it from Tara. I wish there was a way that Connor won't feel bad when he learns his part in it, but I don't see a way around it. We've never lied to each other, and I won't start now.

I flop down on my bed, more tired than I ever remember being. Bone tired. I close my eyes and am instantly in my garden. I didn't even have to use the elevator this time. As soon as I smell the fruit trees, I'm wide awake. Then I'm laughing. The garden has been busy since my last visit!

Every piece of land not taken up by a tree or flower or sand or sea is now home to one of the objects that had disappeared from Angelina's store. If this were my bedroom, my mom would freak out until I cleaned it. But it's not my bedroom, and no one else can find this place.

Well, except Angelina, who seems to have an all-access pass to my brain. I look around, hoping she's hiding behind a lampshade or a faded watercolor painting of a fruit bowl, but I don't see any sign of her. I wonder if she knows about shutting down the vortex, and if she does, I hope she understands why I did it.

A bag of seeds appears on top of a rosebush, or perhaps it was always there and I never noticed it. It's identical to the one left for me on the counter at the store. I carefully untangle it from the thorny branches and slip it into my pocket. I'm curious to see if it makes it back to the real world. Or the waking world. Or whatever the difference is between *here* and *there*.

Before I find out, though, I take one last look around at all the stuff filling up the garden. Looks like I'll have a lifetime to make my way through "wonders unimagined."

But first I'm kinda in the mood for pizza.

Chapter Seventeen

GRACE

Thirty years later

The animals carved in the smooth bark are still visible, their shapes blurred from decades of weather. How young we were the day that I drew mine. How much responsibility we had. How lucky we were to have one another.

I reach out and run my finger over the lion. How lucky we still are.

"I like what you've done with the place," a voice says from behind me.

I whirl around, the last of the seeds in my hands falling to the earth. Not ten feet away, Angelina D'Angelo sits on the stone bench beside the labyrinth, a wooden cane at her side. I have not seen her in nearly thirty years.

"Is it really you?" I ask, afraid to even move. Can she possibly still be alive?

"You've gotten taller," is her only response.

"I've grown up."

"So you have. You all have."

I gesture down the hill, to the big tent beside the apple trees. "Have you seen the others? Tara and David's son is having his bar mitzvah in a few minutes. Can you believe it? We all came back for it. Amanda and Leo are down there, Rory and her family. Connor. I know they would all love to see you."

She smiles, and her duck-shaped birthmark wiggles. I can still spot it hidden in the folds of her many wrinkles. She looks old. She looked old when I was a child of course, but now she looks truly old. Ancient, even. And tired.

"I saw them," she says. "They didn't see me. That's the way it should be." She uses the cane to stand up from the bench. I am struck by how small she is.

"That was very brave what you did," she says, "shutting down the vortex, giving up the long life that was your due, and of course relinquishing your powers. Well, most of them, right?" She says that last part with a wink.

My suspicions were correct all those years ago. She had kept some, too. "Yes, most of them," I reply with my own sly grin. "But really, I had to shut it down. I didn't have a choice. I couldn't let it undo everything you'd done. Everything we'd done."

"We always have a choice," she says firmly. "I doubt I would have been brave enough to choose as you did."

"You were braver than anyone," I assure her.

She tilts her head at me. "You are a scientist now?"

"Yes, a physicist. I research quantum theory. That's the study of how subatomic particles —"

She cuts me off. "You study the nature of reality."

I smile. "Yes."

"How sneaky," she says, but I can tell she's pleased.

I laugh. "Yes. I may have a little more insight into it than most people in my field. Where have you been all these years, Angelina?"

"Oh, I got around," she says. "Mostly I visited other vortexes. I was drawn to them, quite truthfully. Sometimes there were people there — kids like yourself — who needed guidance."

"Did you put them all in comas on their tenth birthday, too?"

She laughs at my teasing. "If necessary!" Then she adds, "Not all of them accepted their destiny and rose to meet it, like you did. And sometimes, there was no one there at all."

"And Bucky?" I look around, hoping against hope that he is here, too.

She shakes her head. "He was a wonderful companion. The most charming fiddler I ever did see. But he got tired. He was ready to go."

I feel my heart swell for Bucky. Or as I knew him best, my great-uncle Bill who protected me when I was a child and gave the best birthday presents. "And you? How are you feeling?"

She smiles. "I've still got a little magic in these old bones."

Laughter and music wafts up on the wind from below. "Come down the hill with me, Angelina. The ceremony hasn't started yet."

She shakes her head. "I'll just sit up here and enjoy the shade."

I step closer and reach out my arms for her. She lets me hug her, as she had on the train platform decades ago. She feels both incredibly frail and incredibly powerful. She changed the world, and so few people know it. There will never be another like her.

"Send me a postcard every now and again, okay?" I ask.

She smiles, pats me on the arm, and waits. That's my signal to leave.

"You're sure I can't convince you to come?" I ask one more time. "David and his son are going to sing together."

She nods. I look around for a car but don't see any. "Well, can I take you some place afterward, then?"

"I'll be fine," she insists. "Go enjoy the party, and your friends. Give them . . . give them my love." At that, she turns away, and I know it's really time to go. I lean over and kiss her on top of her head. Then I hurry back toward the party.

I make it as far as the edge of the clearing before turning back around. Angelina is standing beside the apple tree in the center of the labyrinth, its branches straight and proud. I can still remember how it looked before, when it was hugging itself. I dare not breathe as I watch Angelina reach out and touch the smooth bark with both hands. I blink, and she's gone.

I blink again. She's really gone. Like, gone gone!

I hear a rustling behind me, and for a second I think, *Oh, it's going to be Angelina, she was just playing a trick on me.* But even before I turn around, I know it's not her. Although decades have passed since I placed the protective bubbles around them, I can still sense the distinctive energies of Amanda, Rory, and Tara. They didn't see what I saw. I don't need to be able to read their minds to know they've come to get me.

We stand side by side, grown-ups with our grown-up party dresses and our busy lives, and together we gaze out at the labyrinth we built three decades ago. I'm sure I'm not the only one picturing our younger selves racing in circles through the trees, finding the perfect stones, feeling the surge of energy when we connected with the vortex. They don't remember what they experienced in those final moments, those glimpses of their futures, but I do. I've kept that secret all these years. Everyone should get to live into their own futures, making things happen and letting things happen in equal measure, as one wise old woman once told me. Where's the fun if you already know how it will work out?

"A lot of old ghosts up here," Amanda says, breaking the silence.

I nod. "And some new ones."

"What do you mean?" Rory asks.

"Tell us on the way down," Tara says, linking her arm in mine. "It's about to start."

A minute later, David and his son begin to sing.

Wendy Mass's birthday books are like a wish come true!

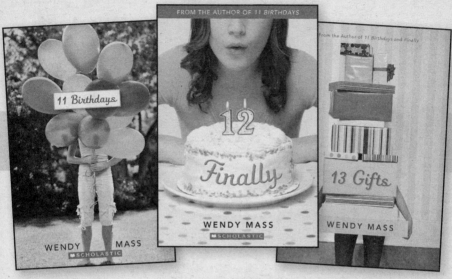

scholastic.com

Available in print and eBook editions

MASSBDAY5

Read the latest books!

donut go breaking my heart
suzanne nelson

Graceful
WENDY MASS
SCHOLASTIC

ANGELA CERVANTES
ALLIE, FIRST AT LAST
SCHOLASTIC

carolyn mackler
best friend next door
SCHOLASTIC

TWICE UPON A TIME
Rapunzel
The One with All the Hair
WENDY MASS
SCHOLASTIC

deep down popular
PHOEBE STONE
SCHOLASTIC

REVENGE OF THE ANGELS
The show must not go on
JENNIFER ZIEGLER
Author of *Revenge of the Flower Girls*
SCHOLASTIC

Natalie
CAROLS AND CRUSHES
SCHOLASTIC

Sealed with a Secret
LISA SCHROEDER
SCHOLASTIC

SCHOLASTIC

scholastic.com/Wish